THE HANGMAN IMPROVISES . . .

Danfield broke from cover and ran up the slope. Tracking him swiftly, Longarm squeezed off a shot. The round knocked Danfield to the ground; he started to slip back down, then hung on. Longarm ran down the slope, across the pass, and was halfway up the slope when Danfield came suddenly to life. He sat up and swung around, a mean grin on his lean, handsome face, and fired point blank at Longarm.

The round caught Longarm in the right side with the impact of a sledgehammer, slamming him violently backward . . .

TABOR EVANS

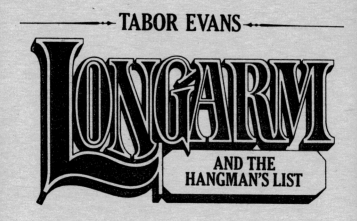

LONGARM

AND THE HANGMAN'S LIST

JOVE BOOKS, NEW YORK

LONGARM AND THE HANGMAN'S LIST

A Jove Book / published by arrangement with
the author

PRINTING HISTORY
Jove edition / October 1989

ISBN: 0-515-10154-0

Jove Books are published by The Berkley Publishing Group,
200 Madison Avenue, New York, New York 10016.
The name ''JOVE'' and the ''J'' logo
are trademarks belonging to Jove Publications, Inc.

PRINTED IN THE UNITED STATES OF AMERICA

10 9 8 7 6 5 4 3 2 1

Prologue

Wade Stripp—thirty-five and unhappy with his growing beer belly—finished his beer and abruptly pushed himself away from the bar.

"Where you goin', Wade," his drinking companion protested. "It ain't late."

"It's late enough, and I had enough."

He pulled his Stetson down more snugly onto his balding head and left the saloon, going out by the alley door, his customary shortcut to his own general store about two blocks down. Unmarried, Stripp lived in a second-story apartment at the rear of his warehouse.

Striding somewhat unsteadily through the night, he found himself forced to push off clumsily from the outhouses that lined the alley. The cool night air had apparently brought the alcohol he had consumed to his head with a rush, and he swore softly to himself, realizing that once again he had drunk too much.

He needed a woman, he conceded, one that would be capable of keeping him to home and out of the gin mills. That's what he needed, all right; but where in tarnation would he ever find any in this town? Most of the available women were Mex, all of them with long fingernails and no love at all for gringos, Texicans especially. Maybe he'd have to do what Alonzo did last year: import an Easterner, a lady who could play the piano and give him plenty of young 'uns. Everyone had laughed at Alonzo when he went north to the Brazos depot to meet her, but when they saw the two of them riding out to their spread after the wedding the next day, no one was laughing, and it was a quiet, thoughtful group of single men who crowded up to the bar afterward.

He reached the rear of his warehouse and mounted the wooden steps to the loading platform. He was about to open the rear door leading to his apartment when the pound of rapid hoofbeats coming down the alley caused him to halt and glance around. Out of the alley's deep gloom swept a rider on a powerful black, his lean, clean-shaven face intent as he leaned forward over his horse's neck, twirling a lasso over his head.

As he charged past Wade, he let the lasso fly. Its loop settled over Wade's head, tightening with a wrenching snap. Wade reached up to pull the rope free of his neck, but before his frantic fingers could dig under it, he was yanked headfirst off the porch. When he struck the alley floor he felt a final, crunching snap deep in his head. A red, smothering blanket fell over him and Wade Stripp was swept, plunging wildly, into whatever perdition awaited his earthly soul.

Chapter 1

Longarm threw the stub of his cheroot onto the tracks and waited for the train to grind to a complete halt. As soon as it did, the conductor hopped down and placed his portable staircase on the platform. Longarm stepped down, pulling roughly after him the sullen, baby-faced felon he had collared in Salt Lake City, and found to his surprise that Wallace and Marshal Billy Vail were hurrying across the platform toward him.

"Wallace here will take your prisoner over to the lockup," Billy Vail told Longarm. "Right now, you and me got other business."

As Longarm unlocked the handcuff linking him to his prisoner, he said, "Now just hold on a dad-burned minute, Billy. What's all the rush? I still got to pick up the rest of my gear in the baggage car."

"Wallace will take care of that."

Grinning, Wallace held out his left hand. With a shrug, Longarm snapped the cuff over Wallace's wrist, and the deputy promptly marched off toward the baggage car, dragging his prisoner after him.

"You mind telling me what this is all about, Billy?"

"I got an assignment for you."

"Can you believe it, Billy? I actually figured that out all by myself."

"Don't go cracking wise, Custis," Vail told him wearily. "This here assignment is important."

"Billy, I ain't even had a chance to warm my ass on a soft seat yet, and already you're sending me out again? What's so all-fired hurry-up about this new assignment?"

"We can't talk here. Come on. Let's go into the restaurant."

The two men threaded their way along the crowded platform, a smaller, chunky Billy Vail puffing slightly in order to keep up with Longarm's easy, loping stride.

Vail consulted his pocket watch. "You'll be having your big meal here in the station restaurant," he said. "On the government." He patted his inside breast pocket. "I got your train ticket and travel vouchers right here. You'll be pulling out on the four o'clock train."

"That's less than two hours! You going to give me a chance to pee, for Christ's sake?"

"We'll both use the lavatory in the restaurant."

"Billy, I'm beginning to smell. I need to lay over for one night, at least."

"You smell just fine. Like a healthy horse."

"I get it. There's going to be another presidential assassination, and Washington wants me to foil it."

6

"Don't get flip, Custis."

Longarm kept his mouth buttoned and followed his chief into the depot restaurant. The waiter seated them at a table by a window that looked out over the bustling train platform.

After they had ordered, Billy Vail leaned back against the leather cushion, an intent, thoughtful expression on his ruddy face. A lawman most of his life, to hear him tell it, he had brought in half the no-accounts in the Southwest, including renegade Apaches and assorted bandidos. But all that was behind him now as he slowly, relentlessly turned to lard behind the United States Marshal's desk, First District Court of Colorado, here in Denver.

Vail's sedentary fate was one that Longarm was determined to avoid, so any momentary irritation Longarm might feel at being sent out too soon on a fresh assignment was always tempered by the realization that, though he might get a little saddle sore, he was not likely to put on much suet.

Longarm took out a cheroot and lit up.

"Let's have it, Chief," Longarm told him as soon as he had his smoke going. "What's this all about?"

"I'm going to have to go back a ways, Custis, to a place called Cool Rock, Texas. Maybe you know the place. It's a pile of adobe huts a little south of the Brazos."

Longarm shook his head. He had never even heard of the place.

"Well, anyway, a little more than ten years ago, a

7

pretty big cattleman in the area got murdered by some rustlers. His name was Big John Thompson. The gang that did it ran off about five hundred head of his stock. From the looks of it, Big John must've come on them when they were rounding up the cattle and tried to stop them.''

''Alone?''

''He was that kind of man. Fearless.''

''And dead.''

''A couple of his ranch hands found him soon after the rustlers had cut him down, and when the foreman brought Big John's body into town, the sheriff swore out a posse and went hunting for the killers. By night-fall they got lucky—or so they thought. They found a cattleman from up north driving a few hundred head of Big John's steers. They hung the poor bastard on the spot.''

''Without a trial?''

''They were anxious to see justice done.''

''I can smell what's coming.''

''You guessed it. He had insisted he bought the steers from Big John, and while he was twisting on the end of the rope, one of the posse members checked the dead man's saddlebags and found a bill of sale signed by Big John himself. The posse let the poor bastard's four drovers go, then rode back to town and tried to find holes they could crawl into. A couple of days later the Texas Rangers caught up with four Mex rustlers driving Big John's stock across the river into Mexico.''

"I suppose there's no doubt they were the ones who killed Big John."

Vail snorted and shook his head. "Not much, Custis. One of the poor bastards was wearing Big John's revolver, another had his Winchester."

"Not a very pleasant story, Billy. But that was ten years ago."

"Keep your shirt on, Custis. I'm getting to it. Three weeks ago in Cool Rock, Texas, one of the posse members, Wade Stripp, was found hanging from a tree limb. Pinned to his chest with a skinning knife was a bill of sale."

"For three hundred head of cattle, I'll bet."

Billy Vail nodded grimly. "This man they hung by mistake ten years ago—his name was Justin Danfield—must've had kin, a son maybe, who's grown up now and coming for them that were in the posse."

"All told, how many were there?"

"Counting the sheriff, ten."

"What about the sheriff?"

"He's been dead long since. Got blown apart by a couple of Saturday night revelers two years later."

"Maybe he was the lucky one. So with Wade Stripp gone, that leaves eight."

Vail shook his head grimly. "Wrong. Three days ago another member of the posse was found hanging from a rafter in his barn. Roger Premo. His wife found him. He had a dagger in his chest holding in place a bill of sale."

Longarm took a deep breath. "I guess that settles it. What have we got to go on?"

"Not much. All I can give you is a partial list of the remaining posse members—four in all—but they and the other three have scattered to hell and gone."

"Damn it, Billy, that means warning them is out of the question."

"It sure as hell is, until we get a line on where they might be. I suggest you start in Montana Territory, where Danfield came from. Look for any kin of his. Maybe a son, or a brother."

"Montana's a big territory, Billy."

"I been doing some work on that. There's some Danfields near Billings, and another passel southwest of Billings in the Absarokas."

"That's not much to go on."

"It's the best I can do, Custis."

Longarm asked no more questions. His meal arrived and he dug in hungrily, the knowledge that the government was footing the bill adding to the tender succulence of the steak. At last, the full-course meal done and a glass of beer in his hand, he rested his head back against the leather and considered the task that lay before him. Some kin of Justin Danfield—a grown son maybe, or a brother—was responsible for two deaths already. And all Longarm had to do was find out who the killer was and stop him before he added more victims to his list. One thing was for sure. This kin of Justin Danfield was doing what he could to alert, and properly terrify, those posse members still alive. There had been no justice at all in what had happened to Justin Danfield ten years before, and each member of that posse was equally responsible for his death. But no matter how just the cause, the law could not allow that fact to temper its resolve.

And neither could Longarm.

He ordered another beer. Vail joined him and the two men proceeded to discuss soberly Longarm's assignment. Vail offered Longarm the benefit of his not inconsiderable advice, the result of his many years as a peace officer on the owlhoot trail. But when it came time for Longarm to board a second dusty train within three hours, he was acutely aware that the man he was trying to overhaul held most of the cards, and that if Longarm didn't stop him soon, seven more men would be found hanging from a limb, a bill of sale for three hundred head of cattle stuck in their ribs.

Longarm pulled his mount to a halt and gazed across the valley at the distant ranch buildings huddled close under a towering, snowcapped peak. It was as if the mountain were a great, crouching cat, and the ranch buildings rested within the protection of its ponderous, timber-clad paws. There were other peaks as well; the valley was enclosed by them. Titanic, snowcapped, their towering height and enormous breadth humbled Longarm.

He was deep in the Absarokas, having spent nearly two weeks in and around Billings looking for any trace of the Danfields. Checking over the back issues in the

Billings Sentinel's newspaper morgue, he had found only two news accounts of the Danfields in the preceding eight years, one having to do with the marriage of the elder Mason Danfield's two daughters, the announcement including the news that both daughters were going to follow their husbands to California. The other news item concerned the exciting news that Mrs. Mason Danfield's grandfather was visiting from San Francisco, and planned to spend the entire summer.

With only these leads to go on, Longarm managed an interview with a surviving member of this local Danfield clan. Mrs. Mason Danfield was a white-haired old matriarch living in a back room of a cheap boardinghouse who took in sewing to make ends meet. She had to be more than eighty, Longarm realized. She and her kin, she said, hailed from Kentucky. When Longarm inquired of any other surviving members of her family, she shook her head sadly, mentioning only her two daughters, who had long since disappeared into California with their husbands without a single glance back. And she professed no knowledge of a cattleman kin anywhere in the area.

Longarm left the old woman confident she had not held anything back. Judging from her present grim circumstances and her brief but telling accounts of the lives of her relatives, this branch of the Danfield clan had only the dimmest possible connection to Justin Danfield and his clan. Hardworking nesters all of them, Mason Danfield's hardscrabble kinfolk seemed singularly out of place in this high cattle country wrested so recently from the Indian and his buffalo.

Close to giving up, Longarm had been slaking his thirst at a Billings saloon he had come to frequent when a man in a black, floppy-brim hat sidled up to him at the bar and waited for Longarm's offer to join him in a drink. As soon as Longarm pushed his bottle toward him, the fellow shook his hand and introduced himself as Caleb Younger, after which he filled a shot glass the barkeep had provided with Longarm's whiskey, and gulped it down greedily. Smiling in gratitude, he directed the full force of his personality on Longarm. Caleb's uneven yellow teeth resembled fangs, while his manner reminded Longarm of a slinking coyote.

"I been watchin' you," Caleb allowed, drawing phlegm back into his nostrils for emphasis.

"That so? Have another drink."

"Don't mind if I do," Caleb said, reaching for the bottle and helping himself.

Longarm waited for him to toss the whiskey down. When he had, he wiped his running nose with the back of his hand and leaned close to Longarm, his grin appalling.

"Yup, I been watchin' you. And I know yer after the Danfields—but not them sodbusters livin' here in Billings."

"Go on," prompted Longarm.

Caleb reached for the bottle. Longarm held it firm, however. "You got me curious, Caleb. If you've got information for me, let's have it. If it's worth anything to me, you can have the bottle.''

Younger's bright eyes flashed greedily toward the bottle, which was still more than half full. "There's a rancher in the Absarokas, I heard. Or was. The other side of Wolf Pass, near Buffalo City. He's a Danfield. Been runnin' stock out there since the Blackfeet.''

"Justin Danfield, is it?''

"He's a Danfield. That's all I know,'' Caleb said, casting anxious eyes on the bottle.

"That's not much to go on, Caleb.''

"There's Danfields out there, I tell you. And one was a cattleman. I been to Buffalo City. I know it for sure.''

"What happened to him?''

"All I know is he disappeared. But there's others out there, kinfolk. I seen them.''

Longarm studied the man carefully. His shirt, coat, and pants were filthy, the tail of his frock coat in tatters, his unwashed smell enough to turn a skunk in its tracks. The man was a lush, of a type only too familiar to saloon patrons throughout the West. All he wanted now was that nearly full bottle of whiskey sitting tantalizingly before him on the bar. In his present state he would be only too anxious to tell Longarm all he knew—but if Longarm pushed him too hard, demanding more than he could deliver, in his anxiety to get that bottle, Caleb would begin to manufacture details, say anything if only it assured him that waiting bottle. It was best, Longarm realized, to be satisfied with the little Caleb had just given him.

Longarm pushed the bottle toward him. "Take it."

Snatching the bottle off the bar, Caleb Younger turned and scuttled out of the saloon.

Reaching Buffalo City two days later, Longarm spent the night in its only hotel and the next day visited the feed store, the barbershop and the general store, finishing the day by patronizing the town's two saloons. Throughout the day, as judiciously as he could, he had inquired about any Danfields in the area, a Justin Danfield in particular. When he was met not only with silence, but with hard, defiant stares, he knew he had reached Justin Danfield's country.

Now, with Buffalo City a half day's ride behind him, Longarm put his mount down the gentle slope and headed toward the ranch buildings on the far side of the valley. He soon found himself splashing through icy, spring-fed brooks, and was impressed by the lush, well-watered grass carpeting the valley floor and far up the broad mountain flanks as well. In places it was so high it tickled his mount's belly. Yet despite the fine graze evident the full length of the valley, Longarm did not catch sight of a single steer.

As soon as he got within a half mile of the ranch, he understood why. No smoke curled from the ranch house's chimney, and it had about it the sad, untended look of an abandoned homestead. Part fieldstone and part log, its grimy windows stared blindly at him. The ridgepole was sagging and portions of the fieldstone had begun to crumble. The bunkhouse next to it was almost completely hidden by the bushes and weeds crowding it, the corral was in miserable repair, and the two horse barns—sunlight gleaming through their gaunt ribs—sagged wearily, like old men in town reaching out for a bench to sit on.

He dismounted in front of the ranch house, draping his reins over the hitch rail. Striding through the tall grass crowding the veranda, he mounted the sagging steps and rapped smartly on the door.

He was not surprised when he got no response. But to be on the safe side, he stepped back to the edge of the veranda and called out, "Hello, the house!"

As he had expected, only his faint echo answered him. He waited a moment longer, then turned the knob and opened the door. Stepping inside, he found himself in a narrow reception hall that led straight ahead to the kitchen. A cricket fled down the dim hallway and vanished. Beside him, a sliding door led into a large room. Rolling aside the door, he stepped into it and found himself in what was known as the sitting room, usually the best room in the house, set aside for weddings and funerals and very special visitors. It had been closed off for decades, it appeared. A dim yellowish light filtered in through the faded drapes.

The sofa, love seat, and two upholstered chairs, their elegant, brocaded style harking back to a happier, more prosperous time, were gray now under a thick layer of dust, as were the footstool, the end tables, and the lamps sitting on them. The rough wood floors were covered with two large, overlapping braided rugs, their once-bright colors long since faded into a dim neutrality. Yellowing photographs hung on the walls like stains. The clammy dampness in the air was like an oppressive spirit inhabiting the room and Longarm had a sudden, chilling certainty that the last time this room was used was when Justin Danfield's coffin occupied it.

He pushed aside another sliding door and stepped into a large L-shaped dining room. A large oak table, eight chairs pulled neatly up to it, dominated the room, along with a fireplace that filled one wall. Leading from the mouth of the fireplace were the footprints of small animals—chipmunks, squirrels, field mice—their tracks crisscrossing the room in an endless web. Longarm proceeded on into the kitchen beyond, inspected it for a moment or two, then found two bedrooms, as dusty as the rest of the house, and a third room at the end of a hallway. Its door was closed. He opened it and found himself in a study.

A cot, two wooden chairs and a rolltop desk was all it contained. He wasn't sure, but there seemed to be less dust in this room. He walked over to one of the windows and reached up for the window shade. Like something alive, it snapped up and struck the roller with the sharpness of a gunshot. A solid beam of sunlight poured into the room, gleaming dust motes dancing in it. He let up the other blind with a bit more care and stepped over to the desk.

Rolling up the desk top, he began poking through the cubbyholes and came on pay dirt almost instantly—letters addressed to a Justin Danfield. Many were brittle to the touch and only by exercising great care was Longarm able to remove the letters intact from the envelopes. One of the last letters Justin Danfield received was from Big John Thompson in Texas. The letter, in Big John's large, flowing penmanship quoted prices for his yearling steers and some breeding stock.

There were more letters, close to thirty, all told, but these were addressed not to Justin Danfield, but to a Mrs. Mary L. Danfield, and then to a John Danfield. Longarm figured John to be Danfield's son, with Mary his mother or some other kin. These letters began arriving a couple of years after Big John Thompson's last letter, and came from small towns all over the West— including Cool Rock, Texas. A good many were from the editors of local newspapers acknowledging requests for individual copies and subscriptions of their newspapers to be mailed to them. The editors were careful to point out that their newspapers would be arriving late and with some irregularity this far west. But this was apparently of little concern to the Danfields.

In addition to the responses they got from newspapers, Longarm came upon occasional letters from informants the Danfields had managed to press into service as they left no stone unturned in their effort to keep track of the posse members.

A large ledger sat upright on the floor, leaning against the desk. Pushing the letters to one side, Longarm lifted it up onto the desk and opened it. Newspaper clippings had been pasted on each leaf. At the beginning of the ledger, the newsprint on the clippings, though readable, was badly faded, the paper brittle and yellowing with age.

The first clipping, dated April 16, was from the front page of a Texas weekly, *The Rimrock Sentinel*. The clipping was an account of "the sad events" of the week before in the neighboring town of Cool Rock. Here Longarm read a vivid account of Justin Danfield's hanging by a Cool Rock posse led by Sheriff Jubal Brookshire, the account following in almost every detail that given Longarm by Billy Vail.

Each member of the posse was listed, and whoever had pasted this clipping into the ledger had underlined each of the posse members' names in pencil.

Longarm pulled a chair over to the desk and began flipping the pages, perusing swiftly a growing number of different dailies and weeklies as the Danfields kept track over the intervening years of each member of the posse. The clippings were of weddings, store openings, obituaries, any public or newsworthy event that left an imprint in the public record. There were gaps of months, sometimes years, but throughout the long march of the years, it appeared to Longarm that every member of the posse had been sedulously accounted for, with the last entry in the ledger pasted in only several weeks before the death of Wade Stripp in Cool Rock, Texas.

Longarm closed the ledger and took one last look through the desk. He didn't know for sure what he hoped to find, but he kept at it diligently, pulling open small drawers and unearthing dusty photographs, rings, old keys.

And finally an envelope addressed to "Grandma."

He opened it and found what he realized now he had been hoping to find: a list showing the name of each posse member, with the name of a town and in some cases a street address scrawled beside it. The dead sheriff's name had long since been crossed out, the line drawn through it with such force the lead point had broken through the paper.

Beneath the list was a curt message: *Grandma, if you don't hear from me in six months, give this list to Gil Martin.*

As Longarm refolded the list and slipped it into his inside coat pocket, he heard a dim, scuttling sound behind him. He whirled, his right hand flashing across his body to his cross-draw rig. But before his fingers closed on his .44's grips, he froze. A toothless old woman was standing in the doorway. She was clutching a double-barreled shotgun in her bony fingers. Both bores returned Longarm's gaze without blinking.

"Forget all about that side arm, mister," the old woman told him, "or for starters I'll blow your balls off."

Longarm carefully straightened up.

He had no doubt this was the "Grandma" John Danfield had left that list for. She was probably also the Mrs. Mary Danfield who had received those first letters years before. It was she, more than likely, who had started that grim scrapbook. And now she had caught him red-handed. She was old, as old as time and just as frightening. And the set to her gaunt jaw and the angry glint in her old, birdlike eyes warned him not to take her lightly.

"You must be John's grandma," he said, smiling.

"And yer trespassin'!"

"Thought the ranch was abandoned."

"Did you now?" Her old eyes went crafty. "I followed you out of Buffalo City. Heard you was nosin' around, looking for any Danfields. And you came right for this place, like a grizzly after a honey tree. You're a lawman, ain't you? No sense in denyin' it. I can smell a lawman a mile away."

Longarm had no desire to fence with this old bird. "That's right. I'm a deputy U.S. marshal."

"What're you doin' here?"

"I want John Danfield—before he hangs any more members of that posse."

Her old eyes lit in sudden triumph. "You mean he's already stretched some necks?"

Longarm nodded grimly. "That's right."

She leaned eagerly closer. "How many?"

"Two."

"Hot damn!" she cried, her gaunt face transformed. Longarm felt sweat standing out on his forehead. There was a chance the old bird might detonate both barrels out of sheer joy.

"This is crazy, Granny," he told her. "Killing those posse members won't bring anyone back."

"Never thought it would," she spat. "That ain't the

point. Satisfaction's the point. And I don't mind telling you, Deputy, right now I feel pure satisfaction. Them bastards killed my son and left Johnny without a father!''

''It was a regrettable mistake.''

''Don't matter,'' she snapped. ''The fact is they killed Justin.''

''Was it you who sent for those papers? Cut out those clippings?''

She nodded grimly, proudly. ''Until Johnny was old enough to do it himself.''

''How old is he now, Grandma?''

''Old enough. And twice the man you are, Deputy.'' She stepped into the study, the twin bores of the shotgun seeming to yawn wider as she thrust the muzzle up at Longarm. Her eyes narrowed craftily. ''I saw you put something in your inside coat pocket. Something you took from the desk. Let's see what you took.''

Longarm shrugged casually and made as if to reach inside for the letter. Instead, he lunged toward the old crone, his right hand knocking aside the shotgun's barrels. The weapon detonated, the buckshot taking out one of the windows. Moving on the woman with sudden, brutal force, he wrested the shotgun from her grasp and flung it aside. She screeched and lunged at him, her talons set to rake his face. He fended her off by grabbing both her wrists and holding her at arm's length. Undaunted, she began kicking out furiously at his shins, screeching like a witch on fire.

Abruptly, she went still, staring wide eyed at him. Then her eyes rolled back into her head. He let go of her wrists. She sagged to the floor, but before she hit it, Longarm gathered her up in his arms and carried her into the closest bedroom. She was as frail and light as a bird, and as he let her down on the bed, he could feel her heart thudding wildly against her rib cage like a trapped animal.

"It hurts fierce," she gasped, "like a vise closin' on my chest!"

"Just lay still. Don't exert yourself. You'll be all right."

"No, I won't," she insisted through clenched gums. "I'm already halfway through the jaws of hell. I'm dyin'!"

Longarm sat down on the edge of the bed and took her bony hands in his and leaned close. "Don't say any more. Lie still."

"Ain't goin' to do no good if I lie still or not. It's all over, Deputy." Beads of sweat stood out on her chalk-white forehead.

"Grandma," Longarm asked, "where's Johnny now?"

"You think I'd tell you!"

"Give me a chance to stop him. You don't want any more deaths on your conscience—or on John's."

She reached up with her right hand and grasped the front of his coat. With surprising strength, she drew him closer. "Who says I don't? That's all you know, Deputy. And don't you worry none about Johnny's conscience, or mine. Besides, you can't stop him. Not now. I taught him myself. I showed him how to shoot. How to track and kill them bastards that hung

23

my son. And he'll do it! Mark my words. He'll *do* it!''

She gasped suddenly as the vise closed relentlessly on her struggling heart. He saw her face contort in pain and leaned closer. "No more talk, Grandma. Lie there as quiet as you can. I'll go ride for a doctor."

"Too late," she whispered hoarsely. "I'm gone."

"That's fool talk."

She shook her white head feebly. "Oh, I know about that strait gate now! Yessir! I'm goin' through it this very minute. But I don't care! Johnny's goin' to finish them up for me. He's goin' to get every last one o' them bastards."

"If he does that, Grandma, he'll join you in hell."

"And I'll be there waitin' for him!"

The vise in her chest snapped shut. She grimaced in sudden, excruciating pain and looked away from Longarm, her toothless mouth clamped shut so she would not cry out. For a moment she trembled on the dusty coverlet like a branch in the wind. Then, her breath rushing out of her in a kind of sigh, she went completely still, her frail remains appearing to sink into the bed. Longarm rested his ear on her chest, listening for a heartbeat. Nothing. Her old body was as quiet as a stone.

He got up from the bed and looked down at the shrunken old bird, fierce even in death. She had looked death in the face without whining or recanting, and was now on her way to hell on greased skids. If there was such a place, she was probably there already, accepting a warm welcome from the devil himself, a greeting she had certainly earned. She had raised and nurtured a killer, then set him loose on nine men, two of whom had already felt his noose tightening about their throats.

But Longarm had the hangman's list now. It wasn't much to go on, but it was a start.

Chapter 2

Longarm found a shovel in back of the bunkhouse and buried the dead woman on a gentle rise behind the ranch house that gave a clear, unobstructed view of the valley, clear to the white-capped peaks beyond. He left no marker, but piled a few boulders onto the soft dirt to keep off coyotes and wolves. He was reluctant to leave the grave site without saying a few words over the dead woman, but then he figured she'd probably have enough to say herself when she marched into hell, without any words from him.

He mounted up, and headed back to Billings, riding in at midday two days later. After registering at the hotel and luxuriating for almost an hour in one of the tubs in back of the barbershop, he walked over to the land office and obtained a map and took it with him up to his hotel room.

Pulling a chair over to the table next to the window, Longarm opened the map and spread it out flat. Then

he took out Johnny Danfield's list and compared it to
Billy Vail's. Vail had listed only four names, while
Johnny Danfield's list contained the names of every
posse member. Longarm discarded Vail's list, and with
his stub of a pencil began to circle on the map those
towns Johnny Danfield had listed alongside the names
of the surviving posse members.

Starting in Cool Rock, Texas, the circled towns
marched northeast through Colorado and into Wyoming. But the remaining towns formed a rough cluster
extending northwest into Idaho Territory. Danfield had
started his murderous career in Cool Rock, Texas, then
had moved northeast to Indian Falls, Colorado, where
he'd left Roger Premo for his wife to find. If Danfield
kept on his present course, it was a good bet his next
stop would be either Breed Pass or Pine Ridge, both
towns in Wyoming where, according to the hangman's
list, he would find posse members Nat Palmer and
Steve Remko. Unfortunately, there was no indication
which man Danfield would go after first, since both
towns were about the same distance from Colorado.
Longarm decided to head for Breed Pass and hope he
guessed right and was in time to head off Johnny
Danfield.

That meant shaking the dust of Billings before this
day was out.

Longarm quickly refolded the map.

Deputy Steve Remko pushed through the batwing doors
and paused in the saloon doorway for a moment to

accustom his eyes to the cool shadows. A poker game was in progress at one of the two back tables, and Remko relaxed somewhat when he realized that he knew each one of the players. Rita was at the other table with a young cowpoke who'd been chasing her for a week now. There was no one else in the saloon with the exception of Bill Johnson, the owner and barkeep, who was in the act of wiping the bar with a towel when Remko stepped through the batwings.

"Afternoon, Steve," Johnson called, reaching back for Remko's whiskey bottle.

Remko shucked his hat back off his forehead and walked over to the bar. Johnson poured him a shot and pushed the glass toward him. Remko nodded his thanks to the owner. This drink was something he sorely needed. An hour on the trail after a fruitless quest out to that squatter's encampment along the river had done nothing for his temper. Those poor-mouthed sodbusters were going to get their asses whupped and there was nothing Remko could—or wanted to—do about it. This was cattle country, and that was that. He lifted the glass to his mouth, tipped his head back, and flung its fiery contents down his gullet. It took just a little of the trail dust down with it. He slapped the empty shot glass down onto the counter and shoved it back to Johnson. The owner had the whiskey bottle ready.

"Anything happen while I was gone?" Remko asked casually, pulling back to him the refilled shot glass.

"Not in this heat. The only things moving are the damned lizards."

"Any strangers in town?"

"Yup."

The question had been asked casually, like the first one, and was a question Remko had asked of Johnson for the past week, ever since he received that clipping from Cool Rock.

He straightened up slightly now and looked squarely at Bill Johnson. "How many?"

"One."

"Drifter?"

"Hard to tell. A cool son of a bitch."

"Cool, you say. A gunslick, maybe."

"Could be."

"Now just what the hell do you mean? Is he a gunslick or isn't he?"

"He's too young for that, I'd figure. A nice-lookin', clean-cut kid, see, with a ready smile. But his eyes . . ." Johnson shook his head and began wiping the bartop again.

Remko fought an impulse to grab Johnson by his shirtfront and haul him over the bar. His mouth had gone dry. Reaching for the shot glass, he noticed with alarm that his hand shook just a trifle.

"He's just a drifter then, right?"

"Maybe. But his iron is sure well taken care of, and it's tied down, gunslick fashion."

Like pulling teeth, getting a clear answer from Johnson. But he had it now, and knew at once who this gunslick was. Remko picked up the shot glass and downed the whiskey. When he lowered it again, the owner extended the bottle to fill it, but Remko shook his head. Close to panic, he was ashamed of himself for reacting this way. This was no time for panic. But it *was* a time for a clear head. It sure as Jesus was.

"How big a man would you say this gunslick was?" he asked idly, glancing about the saloon's interior casually, as if the answer to his question was not particularly important to him.

"Six feet, maybe."

"Quiet?"

"Like a coiled spring."

"How was he dressed?"

"Red shirt, vest and Levi's. A black, low-crowned Stetson. Dusty, but neat. Asked where he could get a bath. I told him Vince kept a tub in back of his barbershop."

"What was he riding?"

"A black. Prettiest piece of horseflesh I've seen in years." Johnson leaned close, his voice low, conspiratorial. "Remko, you think this gunslick was called in by the Circle O and the other cattlemen to drive out them nesters?"

Remko forced himself to shrug carelessly. "Hell, Bill, who knows what them crazy bastards are up to? And it ain't none of my business till someone makes a move."

Johnson pulled back and straightened up. "Why sure, Steve. Don't get me wrong. I ain't sidin' with no sodbusters."

One of the cowpokes at the poker table whooped suddenly and slapped his hand down sharply onto the card table. Remko spun quickly in the direction of the sound, his right hand already closing around his six-gun's grips. He took a deep breath to calm himself, then looked back at the barkeep.

"Noisy son of a bitch, ain't he?"

"Sure, Steve," Johnson said, frowning slightly at Remko's overreaction. "But that's only Jim Walls. You know him. Loud as a coyote at sundown, but he don't mean no harm."

Remko nodded. His knees were weak. He wanted to piss and sit down all at the same time. "Pour me another shot," he told Johnson. "Think I'll sit down for a while."

Johnson poured and Remko took the glass over to a table against the wall and sat with his back to the wall, facing the batwings. Chinks of gleaming sunlight showed through the slats and dug into his trail-weary eyes, but he did not divert them. He sipped at his whiskey, then called across the floor to Johnson.

"What time did you say that feller on the black rode in?"

"I didn't, Steve."

"Well, when, damn it?"

"A little after two, I'd say."

The barkeep continued polishing the bar, and Remko went back to sipping his whiskey. He wanted to fling it down his gullet and pour himself another quick one, but he was acutely aware how dangerous that would be. He pulled out his pocket watch. It was a little after three. Plenty of time for that bastard to take his bath and find a room at the hotel. Maybe he'd be returning here to the saloon to look for him.

But hell, he could just as easily have been watching him ride in a few minutes ago. . . .

Settle down, he told himself. *You don't know for sure this stranger is the same son of a bitch who killed Wade. And even if he is, he don't yet know you by sight.*

With trembling fingers, Remko pulled the tobacco pouch from his vest pocket and took from it the newspaper clipping he'd received from Cool Rock a week ago. His cousin Jake had sent it to him without comment. And none was needed. It told the story with terrible clarity. One of Justin Danfield's kin was after those members of the posse still living. Like a man running his tongue over a loose tooth, Remko read the clipping again, shuddering as he thought of Wade Stripp hanging from that tree, a bill of sale for three hundred head of cattle nailed to his chest with a knife.

He refolded the clipping and placed it back into his tobacco pouch. He should have lit out the day he got it. But that was not something a man his age did lightly. He had a good job in this prosperous cattle town, and the widow Tallow had been making pleasant sounds lately, offering to let him move in with her permanent, even making him part owner of her boardinghouse. If he took her up on it, he would've found a safe haven at last, a place to grow old in.

But that wasn't to be. He had to keep moving. It didn't really matter if this here stranger in town wasn't

Danfield's kin. The son of a bitch would get here eventually, and while Remko stayed in this town, he was a sitting duck; he'd be sleeping with a gun under his pillow; every shadow would make him jump; he'd become as skittish as a colt. What he needed was a sidekick to watch his back.

And that meant Nat Palmer.

The two of them could stop this crazy son of a bitch before he killed any more of them. Remko would light out tonight and join up with Nat. It was his best chance.

Hell, it was his *only* chance.

This decision made, Remko felt immediately better. He finished his whiskey, and with a quick wave at Johnson left his table and started from the place. He didn't stop at the bar to settle up. He didn't need to. His money was no good in here. Pausing at a poker table to watch the game, he stood in such a way as to give him a clear view of the batwings. After exchanging a few bantering remarks with the players, he moved casually out the saloon's back door into the alley.

It was shadowed and cool out here, the sky a bright blue slash overhead. He heard a few of Fat Sal's girls in the kitchen fixing their late afternoon breakfast. As he walked along the back alley toward his room, he kept an eye on his tail to make sure that he wasn't being followed. When a horse and rider blocked out the far end of the alley for a moment, he flattened himself against a wall, his iron jumping into his hand. But the rider moved on and Remko cursed himself for his skittishness.

No doubt about it, before he got any jumpier he'd better get the hell out of town and warn Nat. Until nightfall then, he'd better lay low in his hotel room.

Johnny Danfield sat quietly astride his black, watching the lone rider he had so easily flushed out of town. The deputy sheriff was riding past a clump of alders, then striking out to the northeast, horse and rider outlined clearly in the pale wash of moonlight flooding the mountainside. As soon as Johnny was certain of Remko's direction, he urged his mount after the rider, keeping to the crest of the ridge.

For close to ten miles Johnny kept parallel to him until, close to dawn, he urged his black to a canter, guided it carefully partway down the slope on the other side of the ridge, and then rode as fast as the moonlight permitted until he reached the pass through which the deputy would have to ride just as the first bright streaks of light appeared in the sky behind him.

He dismounted above the narrow trail that wound through the pass, tied his black to a sapling, and withdrew his Winchester from its scabbard. Then he lifted his lariat off the saddle horn and angled down the slope until he reached a clump of scrub pine not more than fifty feet above the trail, a vantage point that afforded him an unobstructed view of the trail for almost a hundred yards in both directions.

He sat down with his back to a broad pine, thumbed his Stetson off his forehead, and closed his eyes.

But he did not sleep.

He had waited too long, come too far, to sleep now. But he rested, allowing his tall frame to lean back against the tree trunk. As he always did at such times, he found himself thinking of his grandmother, a woman as ancient and as implacable as time, one who had spared no labor in sharpening him like a fine knife, in making him ready for this mission.

Get them, my young tiger, get them all, each and every one of them. First, let them know what is coming. Then let them feel the rope tightening around their gullet. Let them feel their legs kicking at the air and hear the snap deep inside their skull. Let the others know, too, that you are coming. Let them sweat in their beds at night. Let them know that soon it will be their turn. Do not rest or look back until you have accomplished this.

She had told him this in a variety of ways, many, many times in the grim, lonely years that followed his father's death. At night usually, when she tucked him in, her white head close to his, her eyes burning with bright, near-mad resolve, her voice low, sibilant, the words etching into his soul. She it was who taught him how to fire his father's Colt and Winchester, and how to plunge a knife deep into the straw men she provided. But mostly, she taught him how to use a rope: to let it snake out silently so that it settled over a man's shoulders before he knew what was happening, before yanking him brutally from his mount, lifting a man clear into perdition.

He saw her old, lined face now, hanging before him

in the morning's light, her cottony halo of white hair framing her head, her fierce beak of a nose like that of some ancient bird of prey, the wild unappeased light in her eyes, a skeletal witch consumed by only one desire—to avenge the death of her only son.

It will be sweet, my young wolf cub—sweet, indeed, for you to drink the blood of those vultures. Your father will look down from heaven and bless you for avenging him. You will see.

Johnny Danfield stirred restlessly against the tree and opened his eyes. Sweet would it be? No. Not sweet. Bitter. Grandma had lied; it was an embittered old woman's lie. But he would still do what he had to do today, as he had in the past, because all his life had prepared him for this and for nothing else.

It was all he knew.

A fresh morning breeze swept down from the peaks behind him, tugging at the unkempt strands of hair hanging below his hat brim. Again he closed his eyes. The call of a wood thrush echoed in the pines. It soothed him, but he did not allow himself to sleep.

The sun's rays had whitened the trail's dust by the time Johnny Danfield heard the first faint click of iron on stone. He opened his eyes and pushed himself upright. After a few moments he saw the deputy sheriff ride into view. Peering up at the high ground above him, Remko kept his eyes shaded with his right hand. He was obviously aware that he could have been followed from Pine

Ridge, and that if he had been, this was a damn good spot for a bushwhack.

Johnny smiled coldly. He had deliberately made his presence known in the town and had watched with some satisfaction as Remko had left the saloon by the rear door and hurried through the alley to his hotel. It had proved what he had expected: that the deaths of the other two, or at least one of them, had been communicated to him.

As Remko passed beneath Johnny, Johnny levered a fresh cartridge into his Winchester's firing chamber. He made no effort to muffle it, and the crank's metal-on-metal clash carried clearly down the mountainside to the rider below.

Remko pulled up abruptly, his horse twisting its neck unhappily at the cruel suddenness with which the bit cut into its mouth. Johnny could see that Remko was close to panic. His iron jumped into his hand as he peered up around him at both slopes. Confident the timber was screening him adequately, Johnny did not move back, but stood where he was, watching. It was clear that Remko did not know whether to dig his spurs into his mount's sides and hightail it out of there or dismount and lead his horse into cover among the rocks.

His first panic subsiding, Remko dropped his six-gun back into his holster. Johnny heard the creak of his saddle as he leaned forward to pat his horse's neck. Remko was telling himself he had nothing to fear, that he had heard nothing. He should not be so skittish. A thin smile broke Johnny's lean, handsome face as he saw Remko take a deep breath, then urge his horse on through the pass.

Johnny lifted the Winchester to his cheek, aimed carefully, waited for Remko to ride another five or six yards, then squeezed the trigger. The reins parted as slickly as if they had been sliced by a bowie. The horse bucked in alarm, then reared, its forelegs pawing wildly at the sky. Remko went tumbling backward off his mount, struck the ground hard and lay stunned where he fell.

Johnny waited. Remko did not stir. This Johnny had not planned. He had intended to crease the horse's neck, expecting the horse to bolt with Remko still astride it. This would have allowed him to ride after Remko and use his rope.

Now he would have to improvise.

Looping his coiled lariat over his shoulder, Johnny levered a fresh round into his Winchester's firing chamber and picked his way down the slope, his lean six-foot frame moving with catlike grace. As he approached Remko, the chink of his spurs roused the deputy sheriff. Startled, Remko opened his eyes and grabbed for his iron. As he rolled over to face Johnny, Johnny stopped quickly, sighted along the gun barrel and fired a second shot. The six-gun went flying from Remko's hand, a finger going with it.

Remko grabbed his shattered hand in an effort to stem the pulsing flow. "I know who you are! You're Danfield's grown kid."

Johnny paused, then nodded.

"Listen, you got to believe me. I tried to stop them from hanging your pa."

"You weren't very successful, were you?"

"I did my best!" the man cried. "You got to believe me."

"No, I don't. Your words to me ain't worth a pitcher of warm spit." Johnny cranked a fresh cartridge into the Winchester's firing chamber.

"You son of a bitch," Remko rasped. "Why don't you give me a fighting chance?"

Johnny moved closer, his handsome face cold. "You mean like you gave my pa?"

"Jesus Christ! I did all I could! I was the one who found your pa's bill of sale in his saddlebag."

"Then maybe I'll let you live."

Remko began to pant in sheer relief. "Oh, Jesus, Danfield. You won't regret it. I promise you!"

"But first, I want some information."

"Sure. Sure. Jesus, whatever you say! What d'you want to know?"

"Where's Nat Palmer? I couldn't find him at Breed Pass. Seems like he moved out. You and him were buddies, so you ought to know. Where'd he go?"

Despite his pain and his great fear, Remko said, "I don't know, Danfield. I'm surprised to hear Nat moved out of Breed Pass. I swear, that's the first I heard of it."

Johnny didn't believe him.

He smiled coldly. "Don't give me that bullshit, Remko. You and him were buddies. You two left Texas and came to Wyoming together. He would've told you if he was moving out of Breed Pass and he would've told you where he was going."

"I'm tellin' you. Nat just disappeared. I don't know where in hell he went."

"My patience is running thin, Remko. Where'd Nat Palmer go?"

"I don't know."

"You're a liar."

"Honest to God. I don't know where he's gone! You got to believe me!"

"No, I don't."

Johnny took a small step back, lowered the muzzle of his Winchester, and blew away Remko's right kneecap. The man's foot went flying out from under him, his face slamming into the ground. Groaning audibly, his body twisting slowly like a stomped worm, Remko clutched at his shattered knee.

"You bastard," he sobbed. "You dirty bastard."

"Where's Nat Palmer, Remko? Tell me, or I'll take out your other kneecap."

"Go ahead," Remko cried in a sudden, fierce rage. "I ain't tellin' you nothin'."

Johnny kicked Remko over onto his back, cranked a fresh round into the firing chamber, and blasted the other kneecap.

"You tempt me," Johnny told Remko softly. "You really do tempt me. But let me remind you—I'll find Nat Palmer even if you don't tell me where he is. I found you, didn't I? I'll find him even if I have to track him clear to Hades. So what're you gainin' by letting me blow your balls away?"

The inexorable logic of Johnny Danfield's words was enough to convince Remko of the futility of holding out. With a miserable groan, he said, "Nat's got his own place. A horse ranch."

Johnny leaned close to Remko. "Where?"

"The nearest town's Sand Creek."

"How many miles from here would you say it was?"

Hanging on to his shattered knees, Remko managed a sudden flash of defiance. "Find that out for yourself, you bastard."

Johnny smiled thinly and straightened up. Then he put the rifle down, shook out the hangman's noose, and dropped it over Remko's head. Remko tried to fight off the rope, but Johnny just snugged the noose more tightly about his neck, then dragged him over the ground toward an old cottonwood. Remko knew what lay ahead and began to curse Johnny, who paid him no heed as he flung the free end of the rope over one of the cottonwood's sturdiest limbs and promptly hauled Remko up off the ground.

Remko's hands, bloodied and ineffectual, clawed frantically at the noose tightening about his neck. Johnny hauled Remko higher, then turned around and walked away from the tree, his shoulder down as he leaned into the rope. Remko's feet lifted still higher off the ground; his screams became a strangled gargle. Without looking back Johnny tied the rope to a sapling, then turned about with folded hands to watch the man dancing on air.

42

● ● ●

Longarm had found no trace of Nat Palmer in Breed Pass, but he had learned from the county sheriff, who had his office in the town, that less than three days before another rider had ridden in to inquire about Palmer. Even though most everyone in Breed Pass knew and liked Nat Palmer, many of whom probably knew for sure where Nat had gone, not a single towns-man admitted to knowing Palmer.

There was something about the cold-eyed stranger no one liked.

The sheriff gave Longarm a good description of the stranger, especially the sleek, powerful black he was riding, and Longarm was pretty certain that this was his man. The sheriff then mentioned slyly that there was a good likelihood Nat might have ridden down to spend some time with his old sidekick, Steve Remko, who was now Pine Ridge's deputy sheriff.

Longarm thanked the sheriff and lost no time in setting out for Pine Ridge. Though he did not mention this to the sheriff, Steve Remko was the third name on Johnny Danfield's list.

Approaching a pass nearly ten miles outside of Pine Ridge, Longarm heard a rifle shot from somewhere in the pass ahead and pulled up to listen. The rifle shot's echo rolled on out of the pass toward him, played about him for a while on the pine-carpeted slopes, then faded to his rear like a distant bowling ball. Squinting into the bright morning sunlight, Longarm nudged his horse on toward the pass. The shot had caused a cloud of crows

43

to swarm from their perch in a tall pine deeper into the pass; they were still in the air, calling out indignantly, as Longarm rode past them.

The second shot sounded.

On a slope above the pass by this time, Longarm snaked his rifle out of his scabbard and urged his mount to a lope. The high ground was uneven, scarred by gravel-filled washes, deep gullies, and pocked with bunch grass. A wash slanted treacherously across his path suddenly, and as his mount scrambled across it and lifted onto the far bank, he heard a third rifle shot. Yanking his mount to a halt behind a huge boulder, Longarm leaped to the ground and, levering a fresh round into his rifle, ran to the lip of a small ridge to peer down the slope.

Johnny Danfield had flung a rope over a tree limb and was hauling a man off the ground. As Longarm watched, stunned, Danfield tied his end of the rope to a sapling. There was no doubt who this hangman was, nor was there much doubt that the man he was hanging was Steve Remko, the one Longarm was riding to Pine Ridge to see. Longarm flung up his rifle, aimed at the rope just below the limb, and fired. He saw a tiny puff as a portion of the rope parted. But it held, and Remko was still twisting slowly in the still morning air, his neck bent at a grotesque angle. Levering swiftly, Longarm aimed and fired a second time. The rope parted and Remko dropped heavily to the ground.

Meanwhile, Danfield had darted for cover, and from behind a boulder on the far slope began firing at Longarm.

One round snipped off a branch a few inches above Longarm's head. Another ricocheted off the face of the boulder Longarm was crouching behind. Peering out from behind it, he saw Danfield break from cover and run up the slope. Tracking him swiftly, Longarm squeezed off a shot.

The round knocked Danfield to the ground; he started to slip back down, then hung on. Longarm ran down the slope, across the pass, and was halfway up the slope when Danfield came suddenly to life. He sat up and swung around, a mean grin on his lean, handsome face, and fired point blank at Longarm.

The round caught Longarm in the right side with the impact of a sledgehammer, slamming him violently backward. His head struck the slope behind him, and the sky exchanged places with the slope as he cartwheeled through brush and over embedded rocks to the floor of the pass. When he came at last to a sudden, bone-rattling halt, his breath was coming in sharp, painful gasps. As he shook his head to clear it, he heard the fading beat of Danfield's horse.

He sat up. It felt as if he'd been stomped by a team of fire horses. He shook his head to make sure nothing had come loose, then felt of his limbs. Nothing was broken. Then, gingerly, he reached in under his shirt to examine the extent of his wound. He was startled to find no break in the flesh and no trace of blood. A quick inspection revealed that Danfield's round had slammed into the derringer he carried in his watch pocket and that the full extent of the damage to him was a painful bruise and maybe a cracked rib. The condition of his derringer, however, caused him to swear softly. The barrel was bent almost to a right angle; for now, at least, it was useless. He was grateful for it all the same. Once again it had come between him and disaster.

Pushing himself to his feet, he walked over to Remko's sprawled form. He did not expect to find the man still alive, but to his astonishment, as he got closer, Remko's eyes flickered open, then began to track him. Noting the sharp angle of Remko's neck, Longarm realized it had to be broken, which made it little short of a miracle that the man was still breathing.

Longarm stared down at the bloodied figure. "Remko?" Longarm asked. "Are you Steve Remko?"

"Yes," the man replied, his voice barely audible.

Longarm knelt beside the man. "Try not to move."

"Shit, man," Remko said, his voice barely audible, "how can I move? I got a busted neck. Who're you? How come you know my name?"

"I'm a lawman. I'm after Danfield."

"I sure wish to hell you'd got here sooner."

"Sorry about that."

"Never mind. Just get the son of a bitch for me."

"I need to know where he's headed."

"He went after Nat Palmer. Nat bought himself a horse ranch . . . near Sand Creek," Remko's voice rasped now like a blunt file. "That's . . . where I was headin' . . . to warn him."

"I'll ride ahead to Pine Ridge for a doctor."

"You crazy? I'm a dead man."

46

"You need a doctor."

"What I need's a bullet in the head."

"That's crazy talk."

"Look at me, for Christ's sake! I got a broken neck. I can't move. I ain't dead yet, but the buzzards won't know that. And they'll be picking my eyes out before high noon. You got to end it for me now."

"I can't do that."

"Damn your eyes!" the man hissed. "If I was a horse, you would! Shoot me, lawman. Then go after that bastard before he gets Nat."

Longarm reached across his waist for his .44, then walked around behind the doomed man, aimed at a spot just behind his right ear, and sent a round into his skull. The bullet smashed through Remko's brain, then ranged on down into his neck cavity without breaking out. Remko shuddered and died.

Longarm had no shovel to dig a grave and the sun had baked the ground to the consistency of concrete. Under the circumstances, he did the best he could. He dragged the dead man into the shade of some rocks, then piled a few boulders on his body to discourage coyotes and other scavengers. But he knew that, at best, he was only delaying the inevitable.

Halfway up the slope to his horse, he saw a vulture's long shadow glide across the trail ahead of him. By the time he had mounted up, another vulture had joined the first. Watching them rocking in the updraft as they dropped lower, Longarm swore bitterly. So far, three men were dead by Danfield's hand, and he had not been any help at all to this last one.

Hell, he had even been forced to finish what Johnny Danfield started.

Chapter 3

Longarm had no difficulty picking up Danfield's trail, and was gaining on him until he lost it in the timbered foothills on the other side of Pine Ridge. He kept on then, heading for Sand Creek, a three-day ride at least, hoping to get directions there to Nat Palmer's horse ranch.

Deep in the timber, night overtook him. He made a dry camp, rolled up into his soogan and was asleep almost immediately, his right hand closed about his .44's grips. As usual, he slept lightly, warily, so that the sound of pine needles crunching underfoot brought him fully awake in an instant. Rolling out of his soogan, he flung up his gun, tracking the clearing behind him. A shadowy figure ducked low, spitting fire. The slug snipped off a branch behind him. Squeezing off a return shot, Longarm crabbed to the right. Danfield sent one more shot in his direction, then vanished into the night. Longarm sent one more shot after him. When its echo faded, he heard Danfield still crashing through the brush.

The night quieted, and Longarm stood up.

The wisdom of moving to a different campsite occurred to him immediately. He rolled up his bedroll and went after his horse. He had hobbled it in a clearing farther down the slope. He couldn't find it immediately and thought the animal, possibly spooked by the gunfire, had moved off despite its hobble. He started to circle the small clearing in hopes of finding tracks and nearly stumbled upon the horse's carcass; in the darkness Longarm could have mistaken it for a pile of wet leather. Kneeling in the grass beside the dead horse, he saw the dark stream running from the slash in its throat. Flies were already beginning to buzz around its head.

Longarm hurried back to the campsite, lugged his saddle and the rest of his gear to higher ground, and with his back to a pine, waited out daybreak. When it came, he cached his saddle and bedroll and set out on foot, carrying only his canteen and Winchester. Evidently, Danfield was in no mood to let Longarm remain loose in his rear, which meant he would most likely make another attempt to take Longarm out.

Longarm came out of the timber a little before noon and found himself crossing a broad gap in the range. Ahead of him stretched a flat, rocky ground running between steep slopes pocked with scrub pine. Wary, he kept to the left slope, moving forward with great caution. Halfway through the pass, the short hair on the back of his neck lifted suddenly. He halted. From high above, a rifle crackled, the round whining off a rock slab to his right. He ducked behind a boulder, and with his shoulders pressed hard against it, scanned the slope above him.

The vegetation was scarce, mostly bushes and scrub pine, its roots holding on with fierce tenacity to the steep, sheer walls of rock. He stayed where he was, hoping for a glimpse of the rifleman. The sun rose higher. But no more shots came, and Longarm caught no glimpse of a swift, hurrying shape.

But that didn't mean a thing.

Johnny Danfield was up there. Longarm could feel the hangman's eyes on him.

It was beginning to dawn on Longarm just what it meant to have as an adversary a young man trained from his youth to track and kill—without mercy. Danfield had revealed as much emotion hauling the hapless Steve Remko into the air as he would have shown hauling a load of hay into a loft. That crazy old woman had created a killer not only efficient, but with no scintilla of compassion for his victims.

Or for anyone who stood in his way.

His sweat-stained shirt was getting heavier every minute, and his eyes were weary of squinting painfully up the slope in an effort to catch a glimpse of Danfield. As he waited, he found himself recalling Grandma Danfield's bony hands pulling him close while her quavering voice hissed that her grandson Johnny would get every one of them surviving posse members. He no longer considered her words the product of a crazed old woman.

The blazing sun tracked higher into the cloudless sky until the boulder no longer provided shade. Its pitiless blast poured straight down at him. Sweat stood out on his face. He was an anvil and the sun was the hammer. It was not long before he drained his canteen. His senses began to drift, and when he shifted the Winchester to his left hand, he did so carelessly. The searing barrel caused him to cry out in startled surprise and he almost dropped the rifle.

He peered out from behind the boulder. A portion of a rock wall less than a hundred yards away leaned away from the mountainside, providing shade to the ground beneath it. In the midst of the cool shadows a small patch of grass beckoned. Just above the grass he saw the gleam of water oozing through cracks in the rock wall. But to get there, he would have to cross a stretch of open ground. He estimated the distance to be at least fifty yards.

It would not be wise for him to attempt it.

On the other hand, to a man frying in hell, paradise is worth any risk.

He glanced once more about him at the steep slopes. Nothing. No sign of Danfield. Perhaps he had left long ago, content to let Longarm fry against that boulder. He inched out beyond the boulder, waited a moment to gather himself, then jumped up and darted across the sun-blasted flat, his eyes on that cool patch of grass. Instantly, the slopes around him echoed and re-echoed as a rifle high in the rocks cracked once, twice, then opened a steady fusillade, creating a thunderous roar that rose in volume until it seemed to fill the universe.

A bullet tore through Longarm's sleeve. Another bit the ground between his flying feet. As he zigged, then zagged, a ricocheting bullet caught the heel of his right boot. He went sprawling. Scrambling to his feet, he flung himself the remaining distance to the rock wall and running full tilt, gained the sweet grass, then slammed into the wet and blessedly cool rock face. But slaking his thirst, he realized, would have to wait.

Flinging up his rifle, he poked his head out from behind the rock slab and peered up at the rimrocks. He saw Danfield. He was racing across a narrow rock ledge, heading for a gap in the giant boulders that sat on the crest of the ridge. Longarm tracked Danfield and fired, levered and fired again. He was still firing when Danfield vanished from sight. In no mood to wait for the hangman's next move, Longarm bolted out of the shadows and scrambled up the slope after him.

When he reached the crest, he darted through the gap in the rimrocks and saw only a worn game trail that led off through timbered foothills to a distant pass. Standing there, sweat pouring off him, he could hear clearly the dim staccato of a galloping horse.

"Shit!"

He saw a dark stain in the dust. Kneeling beside it, he tested it with his finger and found it still damp, despite the sun's direct rays. No doubt about it. Johnny Danfield was human, after all. He bled like any other man.

Longarm got to his feet, following Danfield's footsteps down the game trail until he came to the spot where Danfield had tied up his horse. On the ground nearby, Longarm discovered another dark stain, this one smaller than the earlier one. Longarm had managed to hit him; the wound not enough to bring him down, perhaps, but sufficient to warn him that his pursuer could sting, also.

Feeling somewhat better, Longarm found a shady spot and examined his right boot. There was a deep indentation where the round had dug out a portion of the leather, but the boot was intact, and the spent bullet had not done any damage to Longarm's foot.

On shanks mare, and with a weary sigh, Longarm continued on down the trail after his quarry.

The roan—a powerful-looking saddle horse—was grazing in an isolated clearing below him. Longarm watched it for a while, wondering if he had the makings of a horse thief. He decided that he did. Besides, the presence of this well-fed saddle horse meant there must be a nester, or even a settlement nearby.

He descended to the pasture and eased himself gradually closer to the roan. When it saw him approaching it flicked its ears nervously, swished its broom tail and edged backward. Halting, Longarm spoke to it quietly, waiting for it to resume cropping the grass. When its head dropped down at last, Longarm renewed his advance, moving very slowly, speaking in a low, warm voice calculated to soothe the animal. Once he got close enough, he slipped past the horse's head, patted him gently on the neck, then swung onto the animal's bare back. For a moment he thought the horse was going to attempt to throw him off. He could feel the animal trembling under him, then planting his four feet solidly as his back stiffened.

"Easy, boy. Easy," he murmured softly, leaning forward to pat the roan's neck.

The horse shook his head and glanced warily back at him, its ears flickering.

"Okay, Broom Tail, no use to get all spooked," Longarm whispered softly. "We're going home. There'll be a nice bucket of grain waiting."

The horse quieted, but remained alert, waiting for Longarm to take charge, almost daring him to do so. Resting his rifle across the horse's neck, Longarm nudged the horse around with his right knee, heading toward an opening in the clearing.

The roan cooperated willingly, as if it had understood perfectly Longarm's promise of oats, and its brisk walk took Longarm on a straight path from the clearing, obviously on its way home. After no more than a quarter of a mile, Longarm caught a glimpse through the trees of the shingled roof of a log cabin below him on the ridge, and beyond that a lush stretch of pasture-land and timber. He kept on until he came in view of a pole corral and a horse barn. The corral held at least a dozen saddle horses, and in a long meadow below it, still more riding stock.

By the time he reached the log cabin, a wiry rope of

a man with a drooping walrus mustache was standing in the doorway hefting a double-barreled shotgun. He was wearing a red flannel undershirt and faded Levi's; his britches were held up by yellow braces.

"Howdy, stranger," the old man said, striding out somewhat crookedly onto his porch. He was a stove-up cowpoke from the look of him. Longarm wondered idly how many broncs had sent him flying over the years.

"Howdy, yourself," Longarm said.

"You ride that roan real well," the old man said, "even without a saddle. Neat trick, that. You must be part Injun. But don't figure on buyin' him. He's prime breeding stock and I aim to keep him."

"Too bad. This here's a nice piece of horseflesh."

"You got a name, stranger?"

"Custis Long, and maybe you guessed: I need a horse."

"Light and set a spell and we'll have a smoke on it. I'm a man likes to deal, even in the shank of a hot afternoon."

Longarm slipped off the roan. The rancher reached back inside the doorway for a rope halter. Descending his rude veranda steps, he slipped the halter over the horse's snout and led him into the barn. When he returned from the barn, he led Longarm into the cabin.

The inside was just one long room, one end a kitchen dominated by a huge fieldstone fireplace, the rest of the interior living quarters. A huge brass bed was set against one wall, its bedclothes a tangle. Longarm could smell the thunder jug sitting under it. There were no curtains on the windows, and only a deal table and chairs close by the fireplace. A huge black wood stove squatted in the corner and roughly constructed cabinets were hung on the wall over the sink. A hand pump provided water.

As Longarm took a seat at the table, the old man poked kindling into the stove and got the fire going under the coffeepot. Then he came over and stuck out his hand. Longarm shook the gnarled hand and found it as tough and knobby as old hickory.

"Name's Palmer," he drawled, sitting across from Longarm. "Nat Palmer."

For a moment back there, when Longarm saw that he had come upon a horse ranch halfway to Sand Creek, he wondered if it could be possible that he had found Nat Palmer's ranch. He had dismissed the idea at the time, and now did his best to mask his astonishment.

"Who did you say you were?"

"You hard of hearin', mister? Nat Palmer."

As casually as he could, Longarm asked, "Thought maybe I detected a trace of Texas in your drawl."

"Hell. I don't make no secret of it. Where you from, Custis?"

"West-by-God-Virginia."

Nat Palmer grinned. "Guess we're both a long ways from home, sure enough."

Nat got up then, poured coffee into two huge mugs, and set them down on the table. "Ain't no honey," he said as he sat back down. "And no canned milk, neither. Ain't been to town for more'n a month now."

"You like livin' way out here?"

"You mean livin' this far from civilization, with only them four-footed brutes for company?"

"Guess that's what I meant, all right."

"Look at it this way, son. When you get troubles, ain't it usually a fellow human who brings 'em to you?"

"You could say that."

"You're damned right I could. Long as I can remember, it was allus other people who picked my pocket. Man or woman, it don't make no difference."

"That's puttin' it pretty strong, ain't it?"

"Now that cottonwood out there," Nat said, pointing out the window, "just grows taller ever' day mindin' its own business. It ain't never cheated at cards or lied or failed to pay a debt. All it does is give shade to them what needs it, and in the springtime it makes a place for birds to nest in."

Sipping the steaming coffee, Longarm was reluctant to contradict the old man. With a smile, he suggested, "Nat, don't you think there might be a few disadvantages to being a tree?"

Nat grinned, not in the least discomfited by Longarm's remark. "You mean when someone comes by with an axe?"

"Something like that."

"Well, now, Mr. Long, I guess maybe you got a point there."

Longarm handed Nat a cheroot. "How long you been here, Nat?"

"Not long. A couple of years, come next September."

Longarm lit Nat's cheroot and then his own, after which he leaned back to wait a minute before mentioning his reason for being in the neighborhood. When he thought the time was ripe, he leaned forward and cleared his throat.

"Nat," he began, as casually as he could manage, "didn't you live in Breed Pass before you moved here?"

Nat frowned, surprised that Longarm should know this. "Well, hell, it ain't no crime if I did. But how in tarnation did you know that? I never saw you in Breed Pass. I would've remembered you if I had."

"I been lookin' for you, Nat."

"Me?"

"Yes."

Nat leaned back in his chair and cocked his head, his eyes suddenly wary. "Now just who in the hell *are* you, mister?"

Longarm took out his wallet, opened it and dropped it on the table between them, badge up.

One look at the badge and Nat's face darkened. "Me? You mean you're after *me*?"

"No, Nat. Not you."

"Then who?"

"I'm after someone who is after you."

"What's that you say?"

"Nat, do you remember a necktie party you were a part of near Cool Rock, Texas, about ten years ago?"

Groaning softly, Nat sagged back in his chair. "I remember."

"Do you recall two of those posse members, Wade Stripp and Roger Premo?"

"I do."

"They're dead, Nat. Both of them. Hung by Johnny Danfield."

"Johnny Danfield?"

"The son of the man you hung. He's grown, and he has a list of the posse members."

"A list? Of *every* posse member?"

Longarm took out the list, unfolded it, and handed it across to Nat Palmer. The old cowpoke had to squint to read the names, but he went down the list quickly enough. His old lined face gray as putty, he handed the list back to Longarm.

"You say he's already killed Wade and Premo?"

"And Steve Remko, too, Nat."

Shocked, Nat stared incredulously at Longarm.

"Remko was on his way here to warn you," Longarm explained, "when Johnny must have caught up with him." Longarm decided it was not necessary for him to mention his own part in Steve Remko's death.

"That makes three of us."

"So far."

"And I'm next on his list."

"I tried to find you in Breed Pass, but you weren't there. I was on my way to warn Remko, but I was too late to do him much good. I tried to nail Danfield, but messed up. He's the reason I'm afoot."

"Then he's nearby."

"Maybe, but my thinking is he's ridden past these

60

hills and is on his way to Sand Creek. I managed to wound him. He'll be lookin' for a doctor. How far a ride is Sand Creek?''

"A full day's ride. I got a post office box there, but I don't ride in more than once or twice a year. And when I go in for my mail, I don't spend any more time there than I have to. I was in there last spring at the auction to sell a few saddle stock. If Danfield's persistent and asks around enough, there's maybe one or two townsmen who might be able to give him a line on me.''

"Nat, did you know Danfield was after you?''

"Nope. I didn't know nothin' about this here Johnny Danfield. Never even heard of him. But I allus knew someday a reckonin' would come to every one of us for what we done to that poor doomed son of a bitch.''

"And that's why you moved up here to Wyoming Territory, then came to light here?''

He shrugged. "Now that I think on it, mebbe so. What I know for sure is I been restless ever since the hangin'. I ain't never slept good since. It don't take much to bring it all back, neither. Sometimes, when I least expect it, I close my eyes . . . and see it happenin' all over again.''

"I was lucky to come on your place like I did.''

"If you hadn't been afoot, you wouldn't've. I'm well off the main trail. It was the roan brought you to me. How long you been trackin' this Danfield?''

"Not long.''

"Does he know who you are?''

"I don't see how. All he knows about me for sure is I happened along and caught him hanging Remko."

"What's that? You say he hung Steve?"

"And those other two he caught."

"Jesus."

"One more thing I guess I might as well tell you. After he hangs his man, he uses a knife to pin a bill of sale to the dead man's chest."

"A bill of sale?"

"That's right."

"I'll bet it's for . . . three hundred head of cattle," Nat said, his voice hushed.

Longarm nodded.

Nat shuddered.

For a while the two sat facing each other, neither one saying a word. Watching the old cowpoke, Longarm saw the stunned look gradually wash from his weathered face, to be replaced by a fierce, stubborn resolve.

"I guess it's about time at that," Nat said finally. "The good thing is I don't have to wait no more. What are your plans, Custis?"

"I figure Danfield's on his way to Sand Creek not only to find some trace of you, but to find a doctor to patch him up."

"You're going to Sand Creek after him?"

"If you'll lend me a horse."

"I'll provide the horse, and then I'll be ridin' in with you."

"Don't be a fool, Nat. Your best bet's to stay here and keep your ass down."

Nat shook his head decisively. "You know what the Greeks said, a man can't never outrun his fate."

"Never could read Greek."

"What I'm sayin' is there's no use you tryin' to talk me out of it. I'm ridin' in with you." He grinned suddenly. "Unless you want to walk all the way to Sand Creek."

Longarm shrugged. "Come with me, then. I welcome your company."

"That's better," Nat said, grinning.

"As soon as you select a mount for me, I'll ride back to where I cached my saddle and bedroll. That shouldn't take long."

Nat got to his feet and went over to the cupboard. Pulling down a brown earthenware jug, he returned to the table and freshened the two cups of coffee with moonshine. Raising their cups in salute, they downed the potent mixture, then left the cabin to pick out a mount for Longarm.

By mid-afternoon of the next day Longarm rode alone into Sand Creek. Leaving the chestnut Nat had selected for him in the livery, Longarm crossed the street to the hotel and registered. After checking out his room, he left the hotel and took his derringer to the local gunsmith's shop to have it repaired. It meant leaving his pocket watch with it, but the gunsmith—an elderly gentleman with sleeve garters and a green eyeshade—assured him he would have the derringer repaired in a few hours.

After a steaming hot bath in the back of the barber-shop, he returned to the hotel and took a seat in a wicker armchair on the veranda and leaned back against the wall. Resting his crossed ankles on the railing, he tilted his hat forward to shield his eyes. Like a large, frock-coated lizard, he basked patiently in the sun, noting every townsman who strode past the hotel on either side of the street. He was looking for the cold, handsome face of a young man not over twenty-two or -three with dead eyes and a jaw set with grim purpose.

When Nat Palmer rode in about an hour later, Longarm did not stir or look aside. Nat led his horse into the livery stable, then crossed the street to register in the hotel. As he mounted the hotel steps, he glanced idly to his left. A barely noticeable lift of his eyebrow told Longarm that Nat had seen him. Since there was no chance Johnny Danfield knew Nat Palmer by sight, Longarm had insisted that Nat not enter town with him and that when he did come in, he was to play only a distant backup role without ever approaching Longarm publicly. To play it any other way would almost certainly give Nat away.

As soon as Nat disappeared into the hotel, Longarm pushed away from the wall, stood up and descended the veranda steps. Earlier, Longarm had noticed a doctor's shingle over the barbershop, with the doctor's office on the second floor over it. Striding past the barber-shop, Longarm cut down the alley beside it and mounted the wooden outside steps leading up to the doctor's office.

The rude lettering on the door read: DOCTOR CYRUS TAYLOR, M.D.

Longarm rapped once on the door, opened it, and walked in. The doctor was at his desk, his head facedown on crossed arms. An empty bottle of whiskey sat on the desk beside him. The doctor was snoring loudly, and his cluttered office was foul with his liquor-sodden breath and the stench of his unwashed body.

Longarm slammed the door behind him, then strode over to the desk. Dr. Cyrus Taylor continued to snore. Longarm lifted the bottle of whiskey off the desk and poured what remained of it over the back of the doctor's neck. Dr. Taylor stirred abruptly, raised his head and looked blearily up at Longarm. Pulling his handkerchief from his side pocket, he dabbed at the back of his neck. The effort seemed to clear his senses.

"A terrible waste of good drink, that," he complained. "I presume you are willing to reimburse me for its loss."

"What makes it so valuable?"

"That, sir, was Maryland rye."

Despite himself, Longarm smiled. "My own preference, Doctor," he admitted.

"Good." The doctor heaved himself up from his chair, snatched his hat off the tree beside his desk, and headed for the door. "The Sand Creek Saloon is just down the street."

"Not now, Doc."

"You don't look like a sick man, sir."

"Never said I was. Now, hold your horses. I got some questions."

The doctor wore no coat, only a stained, shiny vest over a white broadcloth shirt. His pants badly needed pressing, an old stain extended from his fly to his knee. The scuffed, unpolished boots he wore seemed too large for his feet. At least six-feet-two, as lean as a broomstick, his gaunt face was dominated by haunted eyes sunken in deep hollows. His uncut, disheveled hair reached to his shoulders.

"Questions?" he demanded, one clawlike hand resting on the doorknob. "What questions?"

"Sit down, Doctor."

Taylor paused a moment, his eyes smoldering. But when Longarm's gaze did not waver, he walked back to his desk and slumped back into his chair, glancing unhappily at the spot where the bottle of Maryland rye had stood. Abruptly he pulled open a drawer and lifted out a stained glass and a tall narrow bottle containing an inky black liquid. Unstoppering the bottle, he filled the glass. At once Longarm recognized the smell of the licorice-colored drink. It was laudanum, a potent mixture of opium and alcohol. The doctor threw the glass's contents down his gullet, wiped his mouth, then glanced covertly over at Longarm, the light in his feverish eyes increasing.

Dr. Cyrus Taylor was not only a drunk, he was an addict.

Longarm pulled a chair over to the desk and sat down. "Sorry I had to lean on you, Doc," he said, "but our business has to be private. Besides, I'm trying to keep out of sight." Longarm took out his wallet, opened it, and held up his badge.

"You're a lawman, are you?" Taylor said. "Well then, what do you want from me?"

Longarm put away his wallet. "I'm looking for a man with a gunshot wound who might have visited you within the past couple of days."

Taylor moistened suddenly dry lips. "A gunshot wound, you say?"

"A .44-40 slug, as a matter of fact. It came from my Winchester."

"And you say this man is a fugitive?"

"He's a murderer. If you want specifics, he's already hung three men."

"Hung them?"

Longarm nodded.

"Surely, you jest, sir."

Longarm sat back in his chair and smiled. It was clear from Dr. Cyrus Taylor's disbelief that he was recalling in some dismay a clean-cut young man he had only recently treated for a gunshot wound.

"Where is he?" Longarm asked.

"I'm . . . not all that sure I've treated the same man you are after."

Longarm described Danfield to him.

"Yes," Taylor said with a weary sigh. "That's the man."

"You've treated him?"

"For a gunshot wound in the shoulder."

"When?"

"Yesterday, early."

"How bad was his wound?"

"The slug tore through the deltoid muscle high on his left shoulder. But he's young. He'll recover full use of the arm."

"And he can still use a gun?"

"A revolver, maybe, but not a rifle. Not for a while, anyway."

"Where's he staying?"

Too quickly, Taylor responded, "He didn't tell me and I didn't ask."

"You're lying, Doc," Longarm said, leaning closer.

Taylor's hand snaked out toward the laudanum. Longarm reached over and pulled the bottle well out of his reach. Taylor flashed a venomous look at Longarm, but said nothing.

"What's the matter, Doc? What're you afraid of?"

"I am afraid of nothing, sir. But this consultation is over. I have no idea where this man you want is staying. Now, I insist you leave my office."

"You know where he is, but you won't tell me. Why, Doc?"

Taylor folded his arms and leaned back in his chair, his eyes blazing, his mouth clamped defiantly shut. Longarm realized then that the only way he could get the information he wanted from the doctor would be to beat it out of him.

Longarm stood up. "You sure you won't reconsider?"

"Good day, sir."

Longarm turned and left the office.

As soon as the door shut behind Longarm, the door behind Taylor's desk opened and Johnny Danfield, his left arm in a sling, stepped through it. Moving quickly around the desk, he went to the window and watched the tall lawman descend the stairs and disappear from the alley.

Then he turned to Taylor. "You told him too much."

"He knew you was wounded. And he knows I'm the only physician in this town."

"You didn't have to say a damn thing."

"Sir, you did not tell me . . . about those men you . . . hung."

Johnny laughed at the fear he caught in Taylor's voice. "Take my word for it, Doc. They deserved it. They hung my pa, for no reason."

Taylor waved his hand distractedly, as if by doing so he could banish Johnny Danfield from his sight. "I want none of it. Or you. I don't want to get involved. I'm a doctor. I treated you for a gunshot wound, and that's the end of it. Get out of my sick room."

"Too late for that now, Doc. You're involved, clear up to your armpits. You got an empty room in back there with a cot and a good view of the town below. And since this here shoulder of mine is still hurtin', I'm stayin' up here until I'm ready to move out. And not a moment sooner."

"I need a drink."

Johnny shoved the bottle of laudanum toward him. Taylor shook his head. "I want whiskey."

"You mean you want to go downstairs to the saloon."

"Yes."

"Sure. Go ahead."

"I'll . . . need some money."

"You spent what I gave you already?"

Taylor nodded.

Johnny Danfield reached into his pocket, withdrew a cartwheel, and dropped it into Taylor's palm.

"Try anything and I'll kill you," Johnny Danfield told him quietly. He returned to the window. "Only don't worry. I won't hang you. I'll find a better way." He turned to look at the doctor as he said this and smiled, his teeth gleaming in his handsome face, his blue eyes like ice.

Taylor shuddered, and without a word he pulled open his door and fled the office.

Chapter 4

Back in his hotel room, Longarm pulled off his stove-pipes and hung his cross-draw rig on the bedpost. Taking the .44 from its holster, he dropped back onto the bed, swung his stocking feet up, and leaned back against a pillow, the Colt resting on his stomach. He was just dropping off when there came a soft knock on his door.

"Who is it?" Longarm called, coming awake fast.

"Nat."

"Door's open." Longarm dropped his Colt back into its holster and swung his feet off the bed.

Nat Palmer entered quickly and shut the door behind him, a conspiratorial gleam in his eye. "I feel like a Confederate spy," he told Longarm. "What'd you find out?"

"Danfield's here. The local doc's already patched him up."

"Where is he?"

"I don't know. The doc wouldn't tell me."

"Does he know?"

"He knows. But he was too busy covering his ass to tell me."

"You think Danfield knows you're here looking for him?"

"He will soon enough."

"The doc?"

Longarm nodded.

"So what now?"

"Think maybe I'll take me a short nap, then pick up my derringer at the gunsmith's. After that, I just might patronize a few of the local saloons. I understand one of them stocks Maryland rye."

"Jesus, Longarm, is that wise? I mean showin' yourself like that?"

"Do you know a better way to draw Danfield out?"

Nat walked over to the window and looked down at the street, stroking his drooping mustache thoughtfully as he watched the traffic. "Guess that might be the best way, at that. Go ahead, then. You won't see me, but I'll be nearby, keeping an eye on you."

"Just don't crowd me. I don't want Danfield to figure out who you are."

"Don't worry none about that," the old cowpoke promised. "I know better than that. But I ain't goin' to let that bastard plug you in the back, neither."

Longarm chuckled. "I appreciate the sentiment, Nat. So why not take a nap yourself? Looks like we'll be up late tonight."

Nat started for the door. "Knock twice on my door on your way out," he said, then opened the door and left.

From the doctor's sickroom window, Johnny could see not only the hotel across the street, but almost the full length of the main street, where most of the town's businesses were located. And all of its saloons. When that fool of a U.S. deputy marshal had burst in to question the doc, Johnny got a pretty good look at him through a crack in one of the door's panels.

He could have taken out the deputy then, and had given it serious thought; but shooting a federal marshal in the doctor's office would have been difficult to explain to the local town marshal. Of course, he could have taken out the town marshal too if it came to that; but these were complications he needed to avoid. His list was still a long one; there were many more stops he had to make yet. And allowing himself to get nailed in this town would not help him make them.

How this federal marshal had gotten a line on him, he had no idea. It was spooky. But the best way to handle the bastard was to use him—to let him lead him to Nat Palmer.

Johnny's left arm was in a sling, his right arm resting on the windowsill as he watched the hotel entrance. For three hours now he had been watching the entrance, waiting for the lawman to come out, and he was getting restless. The doc had not returned in all that time, and

73

Johnny assumed he was sprawled facedown in a ditch somewhere, awash in his own vomit.

Abruptly, Johnny's patience was rewarded.

The U.S. deputy marshal stepped out onto the hotel's veranda, lit a cheroot, then descended the veranda steps and started down the street. Instead of keeping his eyes on the big lawman, Johnny watched the hotel entrance. A woman with a parasol hurried out after the deputy marshal and crossed the street, disappearing from Johnny's line of sight. A moment later an old cowpoke with a drooping mustache left the hotel, glanced after the deputy for a moment, then, with some hesitation, followed after him.

No one else left the hotel.

Johnny kept his eyes on the old cowpoke. His Levi's were held up by yellow braces and he walked the way a man would who had broken a few too many wild horses in his time. And he was the right age for Nat Palmer. Ahead of the cowpoke, the deputy entered the gunsmith shop. The cowpoke walked on past the shop and seemed about to enter the saloon next door. Instead, he kept on past it, pulling up in front of a tobacco shop. Leaning back against the building, he built himself a smoke, his eyes never wavering from the entrance of the gunsmith shop.

Not long after, the lawman left the shop, consulted his pocket watch, then strode into the saloon next door. The old cowpoke waited only a few seconds, then flicked his smoke into the street and followed the deputy into the saloon.

Johnny nodded, pleased. His hunch had been a good one. He had found Nat Palmer. Now, all he had to do was separate him from that tall drink of water and string him up.

He slipped the sling over his neck and tossed it onto his cot. He grimaced as he tried to use his left arm, the pain in his shoulder almost—but not quite—disabling. He left the room, took a generous swig from the bottle of laudanum on the doc's desk, and felt better immediately.

Abruptly, the door opened and the doc lurched in, his face grim with determination. Pulling up in front of Johnny, he took a huge Navy Colt from his belt and aimed it shakily at him.

"I don't like you, Danfield," the doc said, his back to the door. "So I don't care if you were my patient, I'm takin' you in."

Johnny didn't like looking down the bore of a gun as big and as lethal as this Navy Colt. On the other hand, his contempt for the doctor was such that he had no great fear of the man, even in his present condition.

"Put that gun down, asshole," Johnny told him, "or I'll wrap it around your skull."

"I'll do nothing of the sort."

"Get out of my way."

"You forget, I have a gun."

"I ain't forgetting it. But if you ain't careful, Doc, you're liable to blow a hole in your foot."

The doc, looking more unsteady by the second, reached out to the wall to brace himself. "No more talking," he told Johnny, his words slurred. "You're coming with me right now."

Johnny made no move to comply as he stared with undisguised contempt at the poor drunken son of a bitch in front of him. Considering his condition, it was a miracle he was able to remain on his feet.

"You want me to go with you, do you?"

"You heard me."

"Where do you think you're taking me?"

"The town lockup."

Johnny assumed a defeated look. "Well, I guess there's no sense in me tryin' to talk you out of it, Doc. Looks like you got me dead to rights."

"You're damn right I have."

"Go ahead. Open the door. Let's get the hell out of here."

Turning, the doc reached back for the doorknob. As the Navy Colt in his hand wavered, Johnny grabbed the barrel, twisted it out of the doc's hand and flung it into a corner. Then he slapped the doc on the side of his face with the back of his hand and came back the other way with his open palm. Stunned, the doc tried to break past Johnny. Johnny grabbed his soiled vest, pulled him close, and kneed him in the groin. With a gasp the doc slid to the floor, clutching at his genitals.

"I warned you not to try anything," Johnny snarled through clenched teeth. "You shouldn't've drunk all that bravo juice."

He stepped back then, and with needle-threading precision proceeded to kick at the slowly writhing body on the floor, concentrating on the head and shoulders, only occasionally shifting his attention to the man's ribs and gut. He kept at it until he was panting and the doc was no longer reacting to the blows. He stepped back and looked down at the sprawled form.

The son of a bitch was still barely conscious, he realized, the doc's fitfully heaving lungs filling the office with his stench. Remembering the man's drunken probing of his own shoulder the day before, followed by his inept, almost botched attempt to cauterize the wound, Johnny leaned over Taylor and spat in his face.

"I know you can hear me, you drunken bastard," Johnny told him, his voice scathing. "So listen good. You're supposed to be a doctor. Instead you're a lush. I might be a killer, but I got a good reason. What's yours? How many poor sons of bitches have you killed while you fill your belly with rotgut? I'd be doing you a favor if I kicked your brains out. So what I'll do is, I'll let you live." He chuckled meanly. "I can't think of a punishment that could be worse than that."

Johnny sent one last kick at the doctor's face. Taylor flipped over loosely and this time lost consciousness completely.

Back in the sickroom, Johnny buckled on his gun belt and snatched up his rifle. On his way back through the doc's office, he plucked the bottle of laudanum off the desk and with one final, brutal kick at the unconscious man sprawled on the floor, he hurried on down the outside steps to the back alley and proceeded down it to the livery stable.

He entered it through the wide rear door. His black looked fit and greeted him with a pleased nicker. The grain bucket was empty. Johnny slipped his rifle into the scabbard of his saddle, which was sitting on the stall divider, and fitted the bottle of laudanum into his saddle roll.

He found the stable boy pitchforking fresh hay into an empty stall. A kid not yet in his twenties, Johnny had heard him addressed as Hank.

"How much do I owe you, Hank?"

"That big black, you mean?"

"Yes."

"Four bits."

Johnny flipped the money to him. "When did you feed him last?"

"This noon."

"No more oats then. I'm leaving tonight, and I don't want him too sassy."

"Sure thing."

Johnny flipped another coin at the stable boy.

"About ten tonight, Hank, I'd appreciate it if you'd saddle the black and bring it around into the back alley on the other side of the street. I'll be in one of the saloons, I figure."

"Which one?"

"I'm guessing the Sand Creek Saloon. But I'll be out in the alley, waitin' for you. Would you do that for me?"

"Sure. I can do that."

"Don't forget to tie the saddle roll on snugly and

make sure the saddle blanket don't have no wrinkles in it.''

''Mister, I know how to saddle a horse.''

Johnny chuckled. ''Good.''

He flipped another coin at the boy, then turned and left the livery stable the same way he had entered.

The hour was late, close to midnight. In the midst of the crowded Sand Creek Saloon, Longarm was at a table playing poker. Watching vigilantly, Nat Palmer was up at the bar, sipping his beer. While trailing Longarm from saloon to saloon this night, he had done his best to keep his beer consumption to a minimum. But despite his caution, his senses were lightening and his stomach was growing a mite queasy.

Kit Wilder, the town marshal, was the only one of four players left at the table with Longarm. For most of the game, the barrel-chested marshal had been on a phenomenal winning streak, with Longarm the only player he had been unable to clean out. When the other players had come up empty and left the game, Big Betsy, the owner of the saloon, had joined them as dealer, proclaiming table stakes for the remainder of the game.

Pulling his beer after him, Nat edged farther down the bar, barely able to keep Longarm in sight above the heads and shoulders of the crowd of spectators surrounding the table. A moment before Betsy had announced that the next deal would be seven card stud, and now, as she dealt, she called out each card, her voice cutting sharply through the crowded saloon.

Nat went up on his tiptoes to see better.

"Well, now, lookee here," Betsy said, slapping a card down in front of Longarm. "Another ten! That makes a pair showing, Mr. Long. Your bet."

Longarm pushed out a pile of chips. The town marshal matched his bet, his beefy face intent.

Betsy slapped a card down before the town marshal.

"Ace!" she told him. "A pair of aces, Kit. Your bet."

The saloon hushed. Everyone watching assumed Kit Wilder was working on another ace in the hole. His broad-browed face still expressionless, Wilder checked his hole cards, deliberated for only a moment, then pushed two of his three remaining piles of blue chips forward into the pot.

Betsy dealt Longarm his last hole card. After peeking at it, Longarm drew his two other hole cards over beside it, then shoved half of his remaining chips into the pot.

Seeing this, the marshal lost none of his assurance, matching Longarm's bet without hesitation. Then he sat back to wait for his last hole card. Betsy dealt it. He pulled the card toward him, glanced at it, his face still impassive. The pair of aces he had showing faceup on the table were still high; it was his turn to bet.

Without hesitation, he pushed forward his remaining pile of blue chips, then followed with the rest of his winnings. By this time the saloon was so quiet Nat could hear the flies buzzing behind the bar.

Beside Nat, a tall, lean fellow whispered, "Don't look like that big feller Long has much of a chance."

Nat glanced irritably at him. "Shit, man. This here game ain't over yet."

"You know him, do you?"

"Didn't say that."

Nat glanced quickly back at the poker game.

Longarm was in the act of counting out his chips. He hesitated for a moment. Pursing his lips, he glanced over at Betsy. "Ma'am, you did say this here's table stakes?"

"Yes, I did, Mr. Long."

Wilder chuckled. "It's a mite late to be askin' that, Long."

"Just wanted to be sure," Longarm drawled as he pushed every chip he had left in front of him into the pot. "I'm staying," he said, "and I'm calling you, Wilder. What've you got?"

"Three aces," the town marshal drawled, flipping over his hole cards.

As everyone had figured, one of Wilder's hole cards had been an ace—in this case the ace of spades. Three of a kind, ace high.

Nat groaned softly.

"Sorry, Wilder," Longarm drawled. "I got you beat, looks like."

Longarm flipped over his hole cards, revealing two tens to go with the two showing. Four of a kind. The onlookers gasped. Sitting on a ten of hearts as one of his two hole cards, Longarm's last hole card had been his fourth ten.

His face dark with disappointment, the burly town marshal flung his cards down and stalked away from the table, tipping over his chair as he went. Longarm got up and swept the huge pile of chips into his hat and followed Big Betsy over to the bar to cash them in.

"See that?" Nat crowed, looking around at the tall fellow beside him.

"No question," the young man replied, shaking his head in admiration, "that big feller sure has poker nerves. He never let on once what he was drawing to." Moving back to the bar, he said, "Let me stand you to a beer, friend."

It wasn't polite to refuse a drink from a stranger, so even though Nat knew he was close to his limit, he nodded. "I'd take that kindly, young feller."

"Name's Smith," the man replied as he waved to the barkeep.

"Just call me Nat," Nat said when the two sweating mugs were plunked down before them. Then he cursed himself for a fool. What in the hell was the matter with him? Giving his name to a stranger! He glanced nervously over at Longarm, who seemed deep in amiable conversation with Big Betsy.

Following Nat's gaze, Smith remarked with a chuckle, "That Betsy sure is some woman, ain't she."

The owner of the Sand Creek Saloon was indeed a handsome package, and big where it counted most. A dirty blonde with a smile bright enough to start a fire and—from what Nat had overheard that evening—with a heart as big as every other part of her. Her most famous endowment was her generous, upswelling bust, which at the moment seemed almost eager to break free of her low-cut, red satin gown.

"She sure is plenty woman," Nat agreed, gulping down the rest of his beer.

In keeping with a time-honored tradition, he spilled fresh silver onto the bar, insisting that Smith allow him to return the favor and join him in a second round. Smith offered no objection, and when Nat's own refill arrived, he drank the mug's contents quickly, anxious now to be rid of this agreeable young feller. With him hangin' on Nat's elbow, it would not be easy for Nat to keep his eye on Longarm.

But as he placed his empty mug back onto the bar, the heavy glass struck the surface of the bar a mite too hard. His head began to spin giddily. He reached out to grasp the edge of the bar. His stomach, all of a sudden, was churning.

"Jesus," he said softly. "I think maybe I just went over my limit."

"Hang on there, old-timer," Smith said, draping an arm over Nat's shoulder. "You ain't goin' to be sick in here, are you?"

"No, I ain't," Nat muttered, terrified of the possibility. "Help me get out of here!"

As the saloon spun wildly about him, Nat felt Smith hustling him past grinning faces, through sickening clouds of smoke, then out the door into a blessedly cool back alley. Breaking free of Smith, Nat staggered up the alley toward the nearest privy. It seemed to tip crazily on its side as he pushed into it. Not a moment too soon his head was hanging over the noxious hole as he puked up his guts. At last, pulling his bandanna out of his back pocket, he wiped his mouth and streaming eyes and staggered backward out of the privy.

Something hard and unyielding crunched down on the top of his head. He spun around under the blow and flopped on his back to see Smith standing over him, the revolver he had just clubbed Nat with gleaming dully in his hand.

In that instant Nat realized how easily he had been tricked. Smith was Johnny Danfield.

Chapter 5

Longarm had seen Nat being hustled past him, the greenish cast to his face telling Longarm why Nat was in such a hurry. Then Longarm glimpsed the face of the man escorting Nat.

"Excuse me, Betsy," he said. "I got trouble."

Two burly drunks loomed in his path. When he tried to bull his way past them, they reacted indignantly and combined to push him back. Unwilling to get entangled in a brawl at this moment, Longarm slipped to one side and ducked past them, elbowing his way fiercely through the rest of the crowded saloon, the jeers of the two men ringing in his ears. As he plunged out into the alley, he saw Danfield bring the barrel of his six-gun down onto the top of Nat's head.

Drawing his .44, Longarm ran down the alley toward Danfield. At the sound of Longarm's pounding boots, Danfield whirled about and fired at Longarm. The round caught Longarm's revolver, ripping it painfully from his grasp. But he was on Danfield by that time and with his left hand, knocked aside Danfield's revolver. Danfield slammed Longarm back against a wall. With his bloody right hand unable to grasp or punch, Longarm could only paw awkwardly as Danfield kneed him in the groin. Longarm sagged down the wall and tried to roll away as Danfield's booted feet slashed at his head and shoulders. As Longarm slumped past Danfield to the alley floor, his bloody right hand managed to palm the derringer from his vest pocket. Following after him, Danfield kicked Longarm on the side of the head.

As Longarm flopped over, he shifted the derringer to his left hand, kept rolling and fired up at Danfield. The hangman bucked and pulled back, as startled as if he'd been stung by a rattler. Longarm squeezed off his remaining round. Again Danfield took the slug. Staggering back, he turned, ran a few feet down the alley and flung himself onto a saddled black he had already tied to a porch railing. Obviously hurting, he pulled the black around and spurred down the alley.

The saloon's patrons were now bending over Longarm, their drunken babble filling the alley. Staring up at their distorted, idiot faces, he tried to tell them to go after Danfield, but all the lines were down. His head throbbed wildly and he could not speak. As Betsy shoved through the ring of faces to bend over him, he passed out.

When Nat saw Johnny Danfield struggling with Longarm, he pushed himself upright and fled down the alley. In his condition, he realized dismally, he could not help

Longarm. Staggering against a wall that seemed to reach out deliberately to strike at him, he crashed to the alley floor. Glancing back, he saw the saloon's patrons spilling out into the alley behind the two struggling men.

Nat pulled himself back up onto his feet as two sharp gunshots came from the ground where Longarm lay sprawled. Glancing back, he saw Johnny Danfield stagger back, then run for his black. He spurred his powerful horse down the alley. A second later, Nat saw the rope appear in his hand.

Under no illusions as to what Danfield had in mind, Nat flung himself about and ran on down the alley in a crazy, drunken weave. He could still hear nothing above the persistent roar in his ears, but he could feel the pound of Danfield's horse overtaking him. A rope settled over his head. Still running, he tried to lift it off his shoulders, but Danfield, already sweeping past him, yanked the noose snug.

The last thing Nat recalled was being flung to the ground, then the feel of the alley floor scraping his backside. High above him, the yellow cusp of a moon vanished from sight. . . .

Longarm came awake suddenly, sitting bolt upright, staring into the room's darkness.

"Nat!" he cried. "Nat, where are you?"

The door opened and Betsy swept into the room, a lighted lamp in her hand. Setting it down on the night table beside the bed, she leaned close.

"What is it, Custis?"

He turned to face her. For an instant he did not recognize her. Then the events of this hapless night swept over him.

"It's Nat I want," he repeated. "Nat Palmer. Where is he?"

She stepped back from the bed, her fingers over her mouth, the quick, anxious frown on her face revealing her distress. "Let me go get Kit," she said.

"No. Tell me. Where is he?"

"Nat? You mean the old man in the alley? The one running from that feller on the black?"

"Yes!"

She took a deep, uneasy breath. "Nat's dead," she told him. "We found him . . . hanging in the alley behind the livery stable."

Groaning, Longarm let his head fall back onto the pillow, no longer able to ignore the knifelike pain deep inside his skull. It felt like something sharp had broken loose in there. He closed his eyes, felt the bed tip crazily under him, then held on as it became a runaway stage, hurtling down a narrow mountain road. . . .

When next Longarm awoke, his head was swathed in bandages and the sun was trying to push through the drawn shades. From the street below came the rattle of wagons and the clop of hooves. Somewhere in the house a door slammed. Dr. Cyrus Taylor was sitting astride a wooden chair beside his bed, his folded arms resting on the chair's back, his chin resting on his arms.

Because he had tipped his hat forward, Longarm could not see his face. He appeared to be asleep. Surprisingly, the man appeared to be dressed in a fresh suit and the stench of whiskey no longer hung over him.

Longarm moved his head cautiously, anxious not to arouse the terrible pain that still lurked deep inside his skull. Detecting Longarm's movement, the doctor lifted his chin off his folded arms, pushing his hat back as he did so. When Longarm saw the doctor's raw, swollen face, he almost looked away.

"What the hell happened to you, Doc?"

"The same thing that happened to you."

"Johnny Danfield?"

The doc nodded.

"You want to explain that?"

The doc shrugged. "I got drunk and tried to take him in."

"Too bad you messed it up."

"Yes, it is. If I hadn't, your friend would probably still be alive today."

Longarm let his head rest back. He remembered it all too clearly now. The poker game. The crowded saloon. The glimpse he had of Johnny Danfield hustling Nat from the place, and then his own fruitless attempt to take Danfield, ending with the hangman's boots slicing into his head and shoulders.

He lifted his right hand and saw the bandage enclosing it.

"How bad is this right hand, Doc?"

"It'll be fine. None of the fingers were broken."

"What about the rest of me?"

"You mean your head?"

"Yes."

"You suffered a concussion, perhaps a slight skull fracture. I couldn't be entirely sure. There was so much swelling."

"Where am I? This is not your office."

"You're in Betsy's bedroom. She has an apartment over the saloon."

"How long have I been out of it?"

"Two days."

An infinite weariness fell over Longarm. He rested back on his pillow and closed his eyes. "Doc, about Nat. When they cut him down, was there anything . . . unusual about him?"

"You mean the bill of sale pinned to his chest?"

"That's what I meant."

"Forget it. When the knife entered, your friend was already a dead man."

"Is he . . . buried yet?"

"Betsy's already taken care of it."

Longarm glanced away from the doc. He could imagine the funeral. There would have been no mourners. None at all, except maybe Betsy, and she would not know what to say over this old man's coffin before they lowered it into the ground.

He blamed himself. It should have occurred to him from the first that while he was setting himself up as a lure for Danfield, he was also setting Nat up at the same time. Trusting Nat to keep far enough back so

Danfield would not notice him had been asking too much of the old man.

"You shouldn't feel too bad, Long."

"What do you mean?"

"Close by where Danfield mounted his horse we found plenty of blood. And there was more on the rope he used to hang your friend. You wounded him bad, looks like. Danfield won't get far losing that much blood."

"He'll survive. He has the luck of the devil."

"He has that, I am afraid."

Longarm's weariness pulled him down like an anchor. He turned his head away from the doc and waved him away. The last thing he remembered was hearing the doc pulling the door shut.

Betsy reached down and peeled the blanket back off his naked frame. It was morning and she was dressed only in a silk print bathrobe. He wasn't sure, but he thought she was wearing nothing under it.

"I have to give you a bath," she said.

"I can bathe myself," he said.

"That so?"

"Sure." He grinned at her.

"You mean you don't like my baths?"

"I love them. But I'm much better now."

"You rode out early yesterday," she said. "And you didn't come back until late. Where did you go?"

"Nowhere in particular. I wanted to see if I could

still handle that chestnut Nat gave me. It took a while, but I managed."

"The doc stopped in earlier. He says you should stay in bed for another week."

"It doesn't matter what that quack says."

"Now don't go talking like that about Doc Taylor. He's been by your side for almost a week, steady. Besides, Custis, he's not had an easy time of it himself."

"He's a goddamn dope addict."

"You don't know the whole story, Long. You ought to hold judgment on him—or any man—until you do."

"All right, tell me. What's the whole story?"

"The doctor is a dying man."

"I'm not surprised, the way he takes care of himself."

"It ain't what you think."

"Then what is it?"

"He has a stomach cancer. It is, I am told, a very painful form of cancer."

Longarm frowned. Betsy was right. This did put an entirely different light on the doctor. Barely aloud, he said, "That would explain the laudanum then."

"Yes, opium is the only thing that can kill the pain. Now, no more talk. If I don't have to bathe you, I can change the bed."

Longarm sat up, steadying himself with both hands as the room spun briefly about him. His head was no longer bandaged and the earlier, intense pain was gone. All he felt now was a dull buzzing in his right ear where Johnny Danfield had kicked him. The doctor had been right about his hand. The damage was minimal.

92

Longarm had full use of every digit. The day before, when he had taken that ride, he'd tried out his .44 and was reasonably satisfied with his performance.

"I should warn you," Betsy said.

"About what?"

"When I was bathing you the other night, I found some gray hairs."

His hand flew up to his head.

"It wasn't the hair up there I'm talkin' about."

Sheepishly, Longarm glanced at his crotch. "Jesus. That *is* bad news."

"You know what they say—use it or lose it."

"You got any suggestions?"

"Well, I was thinkin' on it some last night going to bed all alone. But I don't think you're up to it, havin' that concussion and all. You'd maybe die on me."

Longarm grinned at her. "A woman with your endowments could kill a man, at that."

"That's not a nice thing to say," Betsy told him, suddenly taking charge. "Get dressed, then go on down to the kitchen while I change this bed."

She turned and left the bedroom. Longarm dressed quickly and was leaving the bedroom when Betsy returned, a fragrant pile of fresh linen in her arms. "I think I liked you better without any clothes on," she remarked, pushing past him into the bedroom.

He descended the stairs and walked into the kitchen. Three of Betsy's dancehall girls, dressed in pink, frilly nightdresses, were giggling over coffee and doughnuts. As he strode in, they sobered, greeting him solemnly.

Longarm knew all three. He returned their greeting and sat down at the kitchen table.

"Any coffee, girls?"

Two of them dove for the coffeepot, while the other went for a cup and saucer. Longarm was well into his second cup when the town marshal knocked quickly on the kitchen door and entered. The girls, used to his presence at this time of the day, set him up promptly, and he was soon sitting across the table from Longarm, a steaming cup of coffee in his cupped hands.

Betsy appeared in the kitchen, shooed the girls out, poured herself a cup of coffee and joined them at the table.

"Betsy," Wilder said, "I was just going to ask Long, here, about this hangman feller, Danfield."

"Go ahead and ask him," she said, shoveling sugar into her coffee.

"Sorry, Wilder," Longarm said. "I don't know all that much about him."

"Any little bit would help," Wilder said. "Who knows? The son of a bitch might ride back through here someday."

"He won't."

"What makes you so sure?"

"I'm going after him."

"For some reason, Long, that fact don't exactly put my fears to rest."

Longarm shrugged. Judging from his recent performance, he guessed he could understand that. He pulled his coffee closer and began to talk. By the time he had finished his second cup, he had told the town marshal and Betsy all he knew about Johnny Danfield. When he finished, the two remained silent for a few minutes, digesting what Longarm had told them.

It was the town marshal who spoke first. "With that list you got then, you know whereabouts he's headin'."

Longarm nodded.

"So where's that?" Betsy asked.

"Idaho Territory."

"This fellow, Nat," Betsy said, "you say he came from around here?"

"In the hills west of here, a full day's ride."

"It ain't that far. But I don't remember seeing him in town much."

"He kept to himself. It was a damn good idea. He had an idea trouble was comin' for him. I told him to stay where he was. I wish he'd listened to me."

"Then he's still got horses up there that will need tending."

"Hell," said Wilder, "they've all run off by now."

"Maybe not," Longarm said.

"I want to go up there," Betsy told Longarm. "Someone's got to take care of them horses. And I want a look at that ranch, too. How soon will you be riding after Johnny Danfield?"

"Today. Soon's I collect my gear."

"Then I'm going with you, as far as Nat Palmer's ranch."

"I welcome the company."

She smiled, leaned over and pecked him lightly on

the cheek. Then she looked over at the town marshal. "You goin' to spend the entire morning in my kitchen, Kit?"

"Hell, Betsy, I ain't finished my coffee yet."

"Then finish it and get out."

His feelings obviously hurt, and a little bewildered at Betsy's abrupt manner, the town marshal gulped down his coffee, mumbled his good-bye, and pushed out through the kitchen door.

"Why don't you see to the horses, Custis, while I clean up these dishes."

He stood up and turned to her. "You mean right now?"

"You got something else in mind?"

"Is that bed up there all made up?"

"Why?"

"I'd hate to muss it up again."

She stepped forward into his arms and kissed him full on the lips. "Now you just let me worry about that."

The bedroom was no longer the sickroom where Longarm had spent almost seven days. The shades were up, the drapes drawn back, and a bright red satin coverlet gleamed like a whore's wink on the bed. Once they were upon it, Betsy made him sit up on the bed while she stripped him, then bathed him completely with whiskey and water. By the time she had finished her ministrations, Longarm had an erection that resembled an overheated Walker Colt. Chuckling at his obvious readiness, she straightened, tossed the whiskey-soaked washcloth into the basin, undid her housecoat and shrugged it off her shoulders. Longarm had been correct. There was nothing under it but her. She let it fall to the floor, then lay back on the bed, faceup.

Longarm joined her, prowling over her, his knees tucked against the outsides of her thighs. It was like coming home after a long cold journey as he feasted his eyes on her. Her breasts were solid and creamy with nipples that lay flat against light pink circles. Her belly was a small, convex mound, her triangular nap, like her hair, a golden brown. Full hips flared sensually into lush thighs, curving into beautifully formed legs. Best of all, this was no gawky, bony girl, but a woman in her prime, ripe with carnality—a woman who knew how to pleasure herself as well as a man.

Gazing up at him, she smiled, her green eyes gleaming. "Take your time," she told him. "Drink it all in."

"You are a lot of woman, and that's the truth of it."

"Now you know what I been goin' through these past days while I tended you. Did you know you sleep most of the time with a full erection?"

"That was a shame, wasting 'em like that."

She glanced mischievously at his thundering erection; then, reaching up, she clasped her hands behind his neck and pulled him down onto her. "So let's not waste any more of 'em."

He felt her incandescent breasts, downy soft, against his chest. She thrust herself up at him urgently as her arms tightened around his neck, flattening her hard nipples against him. He sank his lips upon hers and felt her tongue moving out, circling, demanding.

She pulled back a fraction. "All those nights, Custis! Make me glad I waited."

He kissed her harder, lips pressing her mouth open wider, and sent his tongue darting into her warm softness, a messenger she welcomed. Betsy's hands grasped his face, pulled him down to her full, creamy breasts, rubbed his mouth against them, her sweet cushions enveloping his face. He caught hold of one flat little pink nipple as it passed across his face, bit gently yet hard enough to halt her.

"Yes," she gasped. "Oh, yes, yes."

He let his tongue circle the flat tip and felt it rise, grow firmer; yet it stayed small and he touched the tiny protuberance again with his teeth. She gasped and her hands tightened about his shoulders. He opened his mouth wider, sucked, pulled her breast in deep, caressing it with his tongue, pulling on it, painting it with his lips.

"Oh, God, Custis," she hissed, roiling beneath him. "Now, now, now! Get yourself in there!"

He nudged the inside of her thighs with his knees. She responded eagerly, thrusting herself open for him. He let his warm, throbbing organ probe the hot, moist lips. She groaned, thrust her hips up at him, her arms tightening like two lascivious snakes around his neck. He eased into her, felt her suck him in deeper. She murmured into his ears, urging him to take her, to pillage her, to plow her deep. Instead, he withdrew all the way and pulled back slightly.

He heard the sob in her voice as she pleaded, then her angry protest as she pounded on his back with her fists. "No, no, no!" she cried hoarsely. "Go back in there, damn you."

Instead, he reached down with his right hand and pressed it on her soft pubic hair, then closed his hand over the mound, feeling it curve upward against his hard palm. She moaned, thrashed under him, thrusting her pelvis at him. As her body lifted, shook, her lips grim with desire, he mounted her swiftly, then drove deep into her, cleaving her, pulled back and plunged again, deeper each time, feeling the hot, moist tightness of her vaginal muscles clasping his erection.

She was totally involved now, out of her head, writhing with steady, building intensity, her head thrusting with grim urgency from side to side, her lips pulled back into a thin line. At last, before he had begun to build to his own climax, she let out a high, keening cry, her fingers digging like fish hooks into his back.

"Ah, ah . . . oh, my God, Custis! I'm coming!"

He laughed and plunged still deeper into her, aroused by the feel of her involuntary contractions. Her cries grew shriller. Her fingers left his back and dug frantically into the back of his thighs. She came then, shuddering from head to foot, pulsing wildly, her ripe body heaving under him. Still inside her, he waited for the storm to subside. But she was in no mood to end this. With renewed urgency, she slammed up into him. Another scream broke from her, shrill, piercing, almost earsplitting.

Afterwards, she clung to him for almost a full minute until the tiny explosions faded and she was smiling up at him, her face flushed, her eyes bright with the excitement of what she had just experienced. "My God," she gasped, "do you think the girls heard me?"

"Only those on this side of the street."

"Oh, my, whatever will they think!"

"It's how you feel that matters."

"I feel wonderful. Oh, Jesus. It's been a long time since it was that good."

"I'm glad."

"But what about you?"

"What about me?"

"You haven't come yet—and I can still feel you inside me!"

"Sure. Remember? I'm not supposed to waste it."

Her eyes suddenly glowed with eagerness. "Let me get on top!"

"Can you manage it?"

Her left knee nudged him. "Roll over."

He did, quickly. She stayed with him, keeping astride him, his erection still snug inside her. As she settled back on it she sighed, and he felt her inner muscles closing still tighter. She blew out her cheeks, smiled like a happy child down at him, then flung her blonde hair off her shoulders. He could see the beads of perspiration covering her breasts. Reaching out, he cupped both breasts with his big hands, his thumbs flicking her nipples.

She pressed forward against his hands, moaning, the tip of her tongue running rapidly across her upper lip. Then she pressed forward, pushing her incandescent breasts against his face, the nipples seeking his mouth. He took them in, first one, then the other, as she began to pump her hips atop him, plunging herself down on him as far as she could go, pressing the inner wall of her warmth against his swollen, pulsing organ, riding him as if he were a bucking stallion, a gasping cry breaking from her each time she plunged down upon him.

He felt her legs grow tight again, stiffen, caught the rising climax of her own orgasm before she felt it. Reaching up, he pulled her to him, rolled back over again, drove deep into her as she let loose with another long, keening scream. He paid no heed as he slammed her into the bed and held his pulsing organ deep inside her, feeling her quiver and tremble as they both came together. Still crying out, her neck arched backward, her entire body lifted under him. She hung in midair as her cry died. She fell back, her arms holding her to him tightly, her face buried in his coiled chest hair.

He rolled gently off her, still holding her.

"You all right?" he asked.

"Jesus. I screamed again."

"Both sides of the street could hear that one."

"Do you really think so?"

"Don't let it bother you. There's no harm in having a good time."

Laughing, she let him pull from her. He leaned back, his head spinning only slightly.

"How do you feel, Custis?"

"A lot lighter, like I just got some much needed exercise."

Betsy pulled the coverlet over them and snuggled closer, and for a while the two just lay in each other's arms, letting the world below the window keep its distance for a while. They spoke softly, idly, about nothing in particular, and for a while time—and Johnny Danfield—were completely forgotten.

At long last, Longarm mentioned something about seeing to the horses and his gear. Betsy sighed and propped herself up on an elbow. "You sure you want to ride out today?"

"I've already lost too much time."

"Take a little nap then. I have some things to do before I can turn the saloon over to my barkeep for the next couple of days. Then I'll fix you a late breakfast and we'll be off."

"Sounds good."

Longarm had already dropped into a deep, satisfying sleep before Betsy closed the bedroom door behind her.

The next day, Longarm and Betsy rode into the front yard of Nat Palmer's ranch. Dismounting first, Longarm helped Betsy down. It was late in the afternoon. They had not spared the horses or themselves. The weather had gone hot with only a short, miserly shower the previous afternoon. Only now, high in the timbered hills, were they experiencing any relief from the heat.

"This is lovely, Custis," Betsy said, gazing about her at the lush, timbered foothills, the long sweep of pasture land. "Now that I've seen the place, I'd be a fool not to sell that saloon and move out here."

"You really mean that?"

"I do."

"Alone?"

She winked at Longarm. "I'm sure I won't be alone for long, Custis."

He laughed. "I guess not."

Longarm spotted about four horses grazing on a distant slope. "Over there, Betsy," he said, pointing at them.

Her eyes lit when she saw the horses. "That means there's more close by, wouldn't you say?"

"Wouldn't be at all surprised. Looks like we got here in time."

"Will you help me round them up?"

"Sure. We should finish by dusk."

"Custis, there's only one thing that bothers me."

"What's that?"

"I'll be takin' this place from a dead man."

"A murdered man. But hell, Betsy, you didn't murder him. And you paid for his funeral. Knowing Nat, I don't think he'd begrudge it one bit."

"I hope not."

"Come on, you'd better go inside and see what that old bachelor left for you to clean up."

Longarm had done his best to warn her about the rough, unfinished interior of the cabin, but when she hurried inside ahead of him, she laughed like a kid and clapped her hands.

"Why, Custis, it's absolutely perfect—just like the log cabin I was brought up in."

"Don't you think you'll be needing to fix it up some? Divide it into separate rooms, at least?"

"No need for that, Custis. I told you. I like it just the way it is."

The soft beat of shod hooves startled them both and they hurried back out onto the porch. Doc Taylor was riding into the yard. He waved once, a mite wearily, Longarm thought, then dismounted and walked toward them, looking a lot cleaner than he had in his office, but no more healthy. As he mounted the porch steps, he nudged his hat back off his forehead.

"Glad I found you, Long."

"Okay. You found me. What do you want?"

"I'm going with you."

"You're what?"

"I want to help bring that son of a bitch in."

"Forget it, Doc. I don't need any more sidekicks. You saw what happened to the last one."

"Damn it, Long. I want to ride with you."

"Why is it so important?"

"I have a score to settle with Johnny Danfield. It has something to do with self-respect, and something to do with making what days I have left on this earth mean something. If I stay back there in Sand Creek, I'll just drown in my own vomit."

"You ain't a deputy U.S. marshal."

"You could deputize me."

Longarm glanced at Betsy. The look on her face told him she hoped he would grant the doctor's request. But it also told him it was his decision to make, that she would not presume to tell him what to do.

"All right, Doc," Longarm said. "We'll be pullin' out first thing in the morning. Lend me a hand while I stable the horses."

Taylor's lean, still-swollen face showed sudden relief that Longarm would take him. His deep, sunken eyes showed something else as well—a bleak determination to get Johnny Danfield, come what may.

Not a bad resolve, Longarm reflected, for anyone on the trail of this merciless hangman.

Chapter 6

Jess Tucker paused in the kitchen doorway. She was sure of it this time. A horse was nickering softly, anxiously from somewhere in back of the barn. And that was not where the horses were. She had let them out into the front corral the night before—unless Abe had moved them for some reason.

She turned about in the doorway and faced the bunkhouse. "Juan!" she called.

A wiry old man, a Navaho bowlegged from his years in the saddle, wearing a bright red shirt and buckskins held up with a white braided sash, stepped through the bunkhouse doorway.

"Where're the horses?" Jess asked him.

"In front corral, where you say, Jess."

She turned back into the kitchen. Placing down on the counter the dish full of chicken feed, she brushed her long auburn hair off her forehead and walked back out through the kitchen door. Abe was lugging a full bucket of water from the well to the bunkhouse. She considered calling him over, but decided against it and continued around back, heading for the carriage barn. There was no horse in sight as she approached the big open doors and she felt a little silly.

And then she heard the nicker again, louder now and unmistakably impatient—coming from behind the barn. She hurried past the open doors and cut through a small tangle of alders. The black was tethered at the far edge of the clearing on the other side of the alders. His massive flanks were trembling and when he saw her approaching, he trotted toward her as far as his reins would allow, then pulled up, nodding his head up and down, ears flat, nostrils flaring.

"Easy, boy," she said, moving close enough to grab its reins.

The horse was still saddled, a blanket roll neatly trussed behind it, a Winchester in the scabbard. The horse had come a long way, its legs and haunches gray with sweat-hardened dust. The horse had cropped all the grass within reach of its tethered snout. She felt the horse's nose. It needed water. That was why it had been complaining. But where was its rider?

She looked back at the barn and remembered its open doors. Hurrying back through the alders, she stepped into the cool interior. As she moved past the second stall, she caught a furtive movement out of the corner of her eye and whirled to confront a tall stranger whose enormous Colt was leveled on her. He was leaning weakly against the side of the stall, and his voice came cold, but soft, just barely above a husky whisper.

"Not a sound, miss. Not one sound."

Jess's hand flew up to her mouth, and she kept herself from gasping aloud. "Who . . . who are you?"

"Never mind who I am."

"What do you want?"

"Where is this?"

"The Lazy J ranch."

"Who runs it?"

"That's not the issue," Jess said stoutly, doing her best not to look at the revolver in his trembling hand. "Who are you, and what are you doing in my barn?"

In the dim light provided by the light filtering in through the dirt-grimed window behind the stall, she could see that the man was frightfully wounded, his shirtfront shiny with fresh blood, his lean face drawn and paler than moonlight.

"Now put down that gun," she continued. "You don't need it with me. I'm unarmed. Besides, you're hurt bad. What you need is help."

He nodded slightly and the ghost of a smile flickered across his gaunt face. Slowly, the movement obviously causing him great pain, he motioned to her to move out of the barn. She could tell his plan was to drive her ahead of him all the way into the house. What he would do then she could only guess. A man in his condition was obviously not going to be thinking too clearly.

Instead of heading from the barn, Jess swung about with lightning speed and slapped at his gun hand. He dropped the gun and staggered back, then reached out to the side of the stall to regain his balance. Then, with a barely audible groan, he collapsed forward. Bracing herself, Jess caught him, but his sudden dead weight forced her to let him sag to the barn floor. As soon as he was resting on the floor, she straightened up and stepped back, her heart pounding in her throat. She could not believe what she had just done, slapping a gun from a man's hand!

Then she became aware of the heavy slick of fresh blood bathing the front of her dress clear down to her knees, and with a small, startled cry, she darted from the barn, crying out for Juan. The Navaho caught her halfway between the barn and the ranch house and shook the hysteria out of her, then led her into the kitchen. As she sat down at the table to recover her composure, the Indian hurried back outside to check the barn.

By the time Juan managed to fling the unconscious man over his shoulder and lug him into the kitchen, Jess had recovered sufficiently to wash the blood off her arms and change into a fresh dress. She instructed Juan to take the unconscious man into the guest bedroom, then followed after him into it. Grabbing hold of the big man's legs, she helped Juan lower him onto the bed.

Then Jess stepped close to inspect him. He had been shot high in the chest and on the left thigh just below the hips. In addition, there was a third, already band-aged wound high on his left shoulder. So many recent wounds aroused in her a kind of dread. Who was this man? And with all these wounds how could he have managed to survive this long? Was he an outlaw, or a man fleeing from outlaws?

Inspecting the two most recent wounds closely, she saw at once that she would have to cut off the red silk shirt and the heavy woolen undershirt beneath it. Dried blood and cloth fragments had become part of the chest wound. Unbuttoning the man's fly with shaking fingers, she pulled off his Levi's as far as they would go and found, just below the thigh wound, a solid carapace of dried blood welding the Levi's to his thigh. She would have to heat some water and bathe both wounds thoroughly in order to soften the scabs and clean them out.

She stepped away from the bed and turned to Juan. "Ride in to Red Bank, Juan. Get the doc. And see if you can find Jim. Tell him to get back here."

"Maybe boss not in town. Maybe he at Circle D."

"Yes," she sighed. "You're probably right. If he's not in town, try there."

Juan hurried through the kitchen. Jess heard the door slam, turned back to her patient and began to roll up her sleeves.

Frank Dannenhower sat facing the open window, feeling the bright sun baking his seamed face. He liked to sit in the sun like this, drinking in the smells that swept in through the open window—especially the pungent odor that came from the sun-drenched axle grease on the old wagon wheel leaning against the side of the ranch house. He could hear the nervous hooves of his broncs circling inside the corral in back of the barn. A ringing

111

clangor came from the blacksmith shop, bringing to his mind's eye a picture of the flame guttering in the bellows's blast and the rippling muscles of his giant of a blacksmith as the man brought down his hammer.

Dannenhower took a sudden deep breath and turned away from the window. No matter how hard he tried, he could not hide his unease. It remained just below the surface of his thoughts, dominating his every waking hour—and too damn many of his dreams. He pulled open the desk drawer under his blotter and took out the letter again.

Dear Frank,

Molly said I shouldn't write, not after you run off like you done, but I told her I'm still your brother no matter what she says. Anyway, maybe you remember Rog Premo. You and him was thick as thieves in the Rangers. He's dead, Frank. Some bastard hung him from the rafter in that new pole barn he built and left him for his woman to find. But the thing is, there was a bill of sale for 3 hundred head of cattle stuck in his chest with a dagger. No one saw the bastard what done it, but I was thinking on it some and what I figure is he might be some kin to that feller you poor bastards hung by mistake back in Cool Rock.

You better keep your ass down, Frank.
Your brother,
Andrew

Reading the letter again only served to increase his uneasiness, but he could not help himself. It was like he was probing at a hole in his tooth with his tongue. Only this was a hell of a lot more dangerous than a toothache.

The sound of two horses cantering into the compound came through the open window. He refolded the letter and tucked it in his pocket, then turned in his chair to see his foreman and the kid riding up to the ranch house. He watched Gulch and the kid dismount, then disappear from sight as they mounted the porch.

His Crow housekeeper, Lilly, knocked once on his door and pushed it open. Her high-cheekboned face as impassive as ever, she told him what he already knew, that Gulch wanted to see him.

"Send him in."

She stepped back out of the doorway and a moment later Gulch stomped in, his hat in his hand. The kid followed in after Gulch, closed the door, and as usual slumped back onto the leather armchair by the wall, his hands thrust deep into the pockets of his gray slicker.

"You got some riders coming," Gulch said as he came to a halt a few feet from the desk.

"How many?"

"Two. And they're both leading packhorses."

This was what Frank had been waiting for, but he was careful not to reveal this to his foreman. Frank did not like his foreman. The man was a slob, unclean and unshaven, with yellowish eyes that made him look sick most of the time. A filthy hat and vest were his trademarks, and usually, after a hard ride, the fat roll of his hairy belly was visible just above his sagging gun belt. But Gulch was slavishly obedient, and Frank was confident that he would never be able to find an assignment too mean, too dishonest, or too dirty for Gulch to be able to carry out. He was a man born to shovel shit for his betters.

"Which way are they coming from?"

"Northwest."

"Good. I've been expecting them."

"You don't want us to hold them up at the gate?"

"You hard of hearing, Gulch? I told you. I'm expecting them."

"Sure, sure, boss. I just wanted to make sure. But there's something else. Juan's here. He's asking for Jim Tucker." Gulch broke into a sly grin. "Guess his wife is getting horny."

"Keep your filthy guesses to yourself, Gulch."

The foreman took a step back, as if he had been slapped. "Sorry, Frank."

"You and the kid take Juan into the bunkhouse to see Tucker," Frank told him, "and before that four-flushing bastard rides out of here, impress on him that I want the money he owes me, or the deed to the Lazy J. Tell him he's got till Friday."

"Boss, Tucker's so hungover, I don't think he can ride."

"If he can't ride, make the Navaho tie him to his horse. I want him out of here. Then ride out to the gate, wait for them two riders, and escort them to the compound."

As Gulch and the kid left, Frank leaned back in his chair, a grim smile on his seamed, hawklike face. For the first time since he'd gotten his brother's letter, he was beginning to breathe easier.

Frank was on the porch when Gulch led the two dust-laden riders into the compound. He watched without a word as the two riders dismounted wearily in front of his hitch rack. Telling Gulch and the kid to take care of their horses and the rest of their gear, he waved them off.

"Good to see you men," he said as they stood in the sun slapping the dust off their clothes.

Lilly had covered the porch table with a clean, freshly ironed tablecloth, on which she had set a pitcher of freshly made lemonade and three glasses.

"Howdy, Frank," said Ned Swinnerton, squinting up at him. "You ain't changed much, and that's a fact."

"Neither have you."

The last ten years had made the tall, rawboned Swinnerton even more stringy-looking, turning his wrinkled face into old leather, his gray eyes smokier. When he took off his hat, Frank saw that little of his once-abundant hair was left. It didn't make any difference. The years had been kind to Ned. He was the same man who had ridden out of Cool Rock with him that night ten years before.

Ned mounted the porch steps and the two solemnly shook hands.

Pete Quirk was Ned's companion. He was still a short, chunky fellow with eyebrows so light it gave his round, baby face an innocent, wide-eyed look so deceptive it gave him an uncanny advantage over his enemies. His gut was bigger now and he waddled more noticeably as he mounted the porch steps.

Sighing wearily, his perspiring face red from the climb, he shook hands with Frank.

"You look all done in, Pete," Frank remarked.

"Hell, Frank. We been on the trail close to a week and a half. Hope to hell this ain't no false alarm."

"No, it ain't, Pete. I only wish it were."

The two men slumped into chairs around the table. Without waiting for any invitation, both of them filled their glasses from the pitcher.

"Your telegram mentioned a letter," Ned Swinnerton said.

"It was from my brother," Frank replied. "I have it here. Maybe I'd better read it to you."

"Go ahead."

Frank took out the letter, unfolded it, and read it aloud to both men. When he finished, he refolded it carefully and waited for comment.

It was Ned who spoke first. "We didn't know about Roger until we got your telegram. But looks like we got something to add, Frank."

"Another killing?"

"That's right," Pete said. "The bastard got Nat."

Frank frowned, trying to place the man. "Nat?"

"Nat Palmer," said Ned. "The bronc buster. You remember him?"

And at once Frank did. "Oh, yeah. I'd forgotten all about him. Hell, he shouldn't even have been there that night. He was one of the last riders to saddle up."

"Well, now he's dead too."

"How'd you find out?"

"On the way here we ran into a drover," Pete explained, "trailing up from Wyoming. Nat was found in an alley in a town there, place called Sand Creek. It was Rog all over again, like in your letter. He was strung up, a bill of sale for three hundred head of cattle nailed to his chest."

"They know for sure who did it?"

"The drover wasn't there when it happened. He heard all this while he was camped outside of town. But the talk was that a tall drink of water forking a big black did it."

"Jesus," said Frank, leaning back in his chair. All of a sudden he was thirsty, but he had no desire for the lemonade.

"That ain't all, Frank," said Ned. "When I got your telegram, I sent one to my cousin in Cool Rock. She wired me right back. Wade Stripp's gone, too."

"Same way?"

"Same way. Looks like this son of a bitch ain't just playin' patty cake."

"Where do you figure he is now, Frank?" asked Pete.

"Wyoming Territory ain't that far from here, and

looks like he's finished there. He's more'n likely heading into Idaho."

Ned nodded and sat back, his gray eyes studying Frank. "On his way to the Circle D."

Frank nodded grimly. "That's the way I see it. Now you know why I sent for you."

"So we just sit here and wait," said Pete.

"Less you got a better idea. I've been sending hands into Red Bank every day to keep an eye out for any strangers. Now, I'll tell them to watch for a stranger forking a black."

"And that's all we can do?"

"That and stick together. Hell, none of us knows what this son of a bitch even looks like."

"Who do you think he is?"

"That's easy enough—some kin of Justin Danfield, his brother maybe, or even his growed son, if he had one."

"Yeah, that sounds like it," said Ned.

"Is the local sheriff in on this?" Pete asked.

"No. And he ain't going to be. This is our fight. We can't afford to let the law get messed up in this. I don't want due process, no trial, and no news items in the local paper. I just want the son of a bitch dead."

"Yeah," said Pete. "I think maybe you got a point there."

Ned nodded, his eyes thoughtful. "I'll go along with that, Frank. Let's get this settled fast without any fuss. I got a life—a good one—on the other side of the Divide, and I want to get back to it."

"We're all agreed then," said Pete, "and now, Frank, would you please for Christ's sake please get us something stronger to drink? It's been a long, dusty ride."

With a short laugh, Frank got out of his chair. It was time for that Napoleon brandy he'd put aside.

Chapter 7

Johnny Danfield woke to the sound of a woman's voice coming from behind him, near his head. Her words were urgent, hushed. She was talking to an older man. He opened his eyes and saw nothing, then realized he was staring up at a ceiling. He turned his head and the woman stopped talking.

She was the one who had come on him in the barn. Her face was round, soft, with dark brown eyes, the same shade as the thick explosion of curls that rested on her shoulders. At the moment her eyes filled with concern as she reached out and rested her palm on his forehead.

Feeling her incredibly cool hand, he became aware of just how warm he was. His lips were so parched they had cracked open. He heard the clink of a crock striking a glass and then she pressed a cool glass to his lips. The water trickling into his mouth was like a revelation. He gulped at it greedily. Some of it went down the wrong way. He gagged, and with each wrenching, gasping cough, lights danced in his head and his chest erupted with pain. But no matter. He must have the water. He finished the glass and lay back content, his eyes closed, the fire within him momentarily banked.

"Can you hear me?" the woman asked.

He managed a nod.

"Then listen. The doc's in the kitchen, washing up. He's going to take those bullets out of you. The ones in your chest and your side. But he doesn't have anything to kill the pain. Only some whiskey."

"The whiskey's fine," he managed.

She stepped back and an old white-haired gent entered the bedroom. He was dressed almost formally, wearing a white shirt, a string tie knotted at his neck. His blue eyes were cool, competent. He obviously knew what he was doing. In his hand he held a bottle of whiskey, and leaning close poured some of it down Johnny's gullet. To prevent himself from choking, Johnny took the bottle in his right hand. The fiery liquid hit his empty stomach like a sledgehammer, its effects almost instantaneous. As his senses reeled, he took the neck of the bottle from his mouth and stared up at the ceiling, closed his eyes, and waited.

The doc began probing the chest wound. Despite the whiskey, a bolt of pain wracked his chest. He opened his mouth to let out a bellow, but all he could manage was a faint moan. He felt the woman take the whiskey bottle from his hand, and then she was pouring a steady trickle of whiskey into his mouth. He gulped at it greedily, praying for oblivion. The room spun about him. He thought for an instant he was going to be sick, but he was too far gone for that.

The doc bent closer over him and probed deeper.

The sun was pouring into the room, falling full upon his pillow and the back of his head. But it was not the sun that had awakened him.

It was the voices. Angry voices. First the woman's and then the man's. The argument was bitter, intense. It stopped abruptly as the sound of a hand slapping a face came to him, followed by that of a fist burying itself into soft flesh. The woman cried out in startled pain.

Lifting his head, Johnny turned in the direction from which the sounds were coming, saw an open door and a hallway beyond. The kitchen, he figured, must be at the other end of it. He could hear the woman crying now, not piteously, but with furious contempt for the man who had just struck her and anger at herself for having let him.

"Get out!" she told him evenly. "And don't ever come back."

"Jess, I'm your husband. You can't kick me out."

"If you don't leave this house right now, I'll . . . I'll ride in and get the sheriff. I mean it!"

"That won't do you no good, woman. The law can't interfere between a man and his wife. So you listen to me. We're leavin' next week for California, and there ain't a goddamn thing you can do about it."

"Go ahead, Jim. Go to California. I won't stop you. But I'm not going with you!"

Johnny heard the woman's muffled cry and the heavy tread of a man's footsteps, followed by the unmistakable sounds of a short, brutal scuffle. In his mind's eye, Johnny could see the woman's upturned face, her tearful, furious helplessness as she tried to release herself from the man's grasp. A heavy saucepan or skillet fell clattering to the floor. The sound of a fist burying itself in soft flesh came again, and this time Johnny heard the woman's bitter cry of desperation and despair.

Disregarding the pain in his chest and thigh, Johnny flung aside the sheets covering him and stood up. He found he was wearing someone else's long johns, but paid it no heed as, using the wall for support, he pushed himself out of the bedroom and down the hallway, wincing with each step. When he reached the kitchen doorway he saw the woman hunched in a corner, her husband doing what he could to pull her from it, probably in order to get a clearer shot at her.

When she saw him, Jess's eyes widened. Her husband saw the look on her face and spun about to face Johnny.

"Well, now, lookee here," he snarled. "If it ain't the star boarder."

"Get away from her."

"What'd you say?"

"You hard of hearin'?"

"You ain't tellin' me what to do. This ain't none of your goddamn business."

Johnny did not agree. As far as he was concerned,

this woman had saved his life; for almost a week now Jess had been waiting on him hand and foot.

"Just leave her be," Johnny said, stepping into the kitchen. "You got no right to slap her around, even if she is your wife."

"Mister, I've just decided. You're out of here. Now!"

"No, Jim," said the woman, straightening up resolutely in the corner and squaring her shoulders. "He's not going to leave. You are!"

Jim turned back around and slapped her as hard as he could. The blow sent her head cracking against the wall. No longer thinking clearly, Johnny lurched across the floor, caught the man about his neck with both hands, then slammed him violently against a wall.

The man stayed upright, clawing at his neck, gasping in fury. "You . . . !" he cried. "You got no right!"

Johnny said, "I heard Jess tell you to get out. So get out! Now!"

"Listen here, you—"

Johnny punched him in the face. The force of the blow spun the man half around. For a moment he held his jaw where Johnny had caught him, then he backed quickly away, clawing at his six-gun as he went. Johnny overtook him swiftly and swiped downward, knocking the weapon from his hand, then punched him again on the jaw. He was half crazed with the delight he felt venting his fury on this piece of offal and swung another looping right, catching him this time on the side of his head, rocking his head back against the unyielding edge of a hanging cupboard. Jim's eyes flew back into his head, and his knees sagged.

But before Johnny could move in to finish him off, he felt a firm hand grasping his right forearm. Jess was pulling him back, tears streaming down her face. What he saw in her eyes—a terrified, stark fear, not of her husband, but of *him*—prompted him to step quickly away from her battered husband. As soon as he did so, Jim sagged to the floor.

"Please," she said to Johnny. "Please! You've hurt him enough."

Johnny looked wearily down at her husband. He did not know whether it was from his sudden exertion or from the wild, ungovernable fury that had swept over him, but he suddenly felt light-headed and as weak as a kitten.

"You told him to get out," he said. "Then I heard him strike you."

"I know," she said, "I know."

Jim shook off the effects of Johnny's blows and scuttled past Johnny and flung open the kitchen door. Crouching in the doorway, he cried, "This won't settle anything, Jess. You're acting crazy!"

"Just get out, Jim," she replied wearily.

"You're my wife, Jess!"

"Yes. And you make it sound like a curse."

"You heard her," Johnny said, taking a step toward him. "Get out."

The man licked his lips as he glared at Johnny. "I

need my weapon. You can't send me out of here without a gun."

Johnny bent, picked up the six-gun, and tossed it at him. Jim dropped it into his holster, looked miserably back at his wife, started to say something, then glanced back at Johnny and thought better of it. Whirling, he left, slamming the door behind him.

A moment later the quick drum of a horse's hooves filled the kitchen.

Slumping into a chair, tears streaming down her face, Jess looked up at Johnny. "I suppose I should thank you."

"You don't have to if you don't want to."

"It's not that, Johnny. Of course I want to thank you, but Jim's such a weak man. All of this is as much my fault as his."

"That ain't none of my business, ma'am, what came before. But when I heard him hitting you, I figured it was time for me to step in. I owed you."

She nodded wearily, pulling toward her a cold cup of coffee sitting on the table. "How do you feel?"

He reached out and braced himself against the table. "You shouldn't've asked. Right now I'm as weak as a kitten."

She got up quickly. "Do you need help getting back to bed?"

He nodded. She took his arm, and with him leaning pretty heavily on her, she was able to guide him back to the bedroom. Once there, he flopped gratefully down onto the bed.

"What you need is some food in your stomach," she told him. "You haven't eaten in almost a week. I'll start with broth first. How's that sound?"

"Sounds great."

He started to ask her about something else, something that just occurred to him, but before he could form the words, he dropped into an exhausted sleep.

Four days later, Longarm rode into Red Bank. He left his mount in the livery stable then walked down the street to the hotel. As he paused in the lobby to light his cheroot, Doc Taylor left the upholstered chair he was sitting in by the window and disappeared up the stairs. Longarm registered and a moment later found Taylor waiting for him on the second-floor landing.

After they exchanged room numbers, Taylor, his eyes sunken deeper than usual, moved on down the hallway and into his room. Longarm entered his own room and dumped his gear in a corner, left his room again, and after a quick knock entered the doc's room.

Taylor was lying full length on his bed, fully clothed, a long, thin bottle of laudanum in his hand. He was pulling on it the way a babe would a bottle of milk. He turned his glassy eyes on Longarm and managed a smile.

"You look bad," Longarm told him, halting beside the bed.

"Funny thing. That's how I feel."

"You going to be all right?"

"Sure. Now I got my bottle. You got any idea where this fellow Dannenhower is?"

"From the clippings I found in Danfield's scrapbook, he's a local rancher."

"He'll be easy to find then."

"Easy enough. I figure we can set out tomorrow morning, early."

"Good. I can use the shut-eye."

"Right now, I think I'll go find me a barber. I smell like a horse."

The doc smiled crookedly. "Out of pure kindness, I had refused to comment on it myself, Longarm."

Longarm went to the foot of the bed and tugged off Taylor's boots, then stripped his socks. Taylor offered no complaint when Longarm lifted his upper back off the pillow and slipped his coat and vest off, then untied his string tie and opened his shirt.

At the door, Longarm paused. "I won't be gone long."

"Watch out for Danfield. That bastard might be here already."

Longarm was beginning to doubt that. Johnny Danfield had taken two slugs at close range. Add to that the fact that his left shoulder had already been torn up some, and it was more than likely Johnny Danfield was holed up somewhere, licking his wounds.

"Don't worry. I'll keep an eye out."

The doc managed a feeble wave, then lifted the long ebony bottle to his lips.

•   •   •

Longarm ducked his head under the steaming water and came up sputtering like a happy seal. He could feel the miles of dust peeling off him like onion skins. He wiped off his mouth with the back of his wrist and pulled a cheroot out of his coat hanging over the chair beside the tub. Leaning his head back against the tub's wooden side, he lit up and closed his eyes. He wanted nothing more than to relax.

And for a while he succeeded, until gradually he found himself recalling the long, wearying ride from Sand Creek. It had not been pleasant watching Taylor's steady deterioration. Though the doc had tried desperately to resist his growing dependency on laudanum, it was a losing battle. And at times Longarm caught a look of pure desperation in his eyes as he fought the insistent, gnawing pain in his belly.

Longarm understood the doc's insistence on coming with him to help nail Johnny Danfield. Taylor had been cruelly used by Danfield, and he wanted the chance to punish and humiliate the man, just as he had been punished and humiliated. But Longarm knew he could not afford to count on Taylor. The doc was too sick. No, he was a dying man.

A shadow fell over Longarm.

He turned his head to see two men standing beside the tub, eyeing him with undisguised hostility.

"I'll be out of this here tub in a few minutes, gents," Longarm told them as he reached for the soap and began soaping his washcloth.

"Just hurry it up, mister," said one of the men. "We ain't got all day."

Longarm turned his head to look more fully at the two men. The one who had spoken was remarkable for his filthy appearance and the odd, yellowish cast to his eyes. His companion was a thin, hungry-looking kid in a gray slicker and a derby hat, who kept his hands in the slicker's deep side pockets.

"I admit you two gents could use a bath, but standing there ain't going to make me move any faster."

"You been sittin' in this here tub for a half hour already."

"You been timing me?"

"Mac told us."

"Who's Mac?"

"He's the barber, you bloody asshole." It was the kid in the slicker who spoke, his voice curiously low, rasping, as if someone had once stomped on his vocal chords.

Longarm decided to ignore them and began soaping his shoulders and neck with the washcloth, preparatory to ducking himself under one more time. Before he could complete the task, however, the tub was overturned, spilling him and the hot, sudsy water out onto the ground.

As Longarm braced himself on his naked hands and knees, the tub was flung aside and the two men advanced on him. His back to the wooden fencing surrounding the bathing area, he waited until they were close enough and lunged, head down, at the unshaven lout closest to him, catching him about the knees and toppling him back to the ground, landing him on his back. Longarm straddled him and punched him on the side of his jaw with a vicious, sledging blow that seemed to take the man out of it.

He flung himself around and was just in time to face the kid in the slicker. He was advancing on Longarm with a blackjack in his right hand. Longarm reached up quickly and caught the fellow's wrist, twisting it cruelly. The kid let out a squeal and dropped the sap. Longarm kicked it out of the way, got to his feet, and grabbing the front of the kid's slicker, swept him off the ground and flung him with brutal force against the fencing. Dazed from the blow, he slid to the ground.

Before Longarm could turn back to the other one, however, he heard the swish of the sap and felt it bury itself into the side of his neck. The rabbit punch paralyzed him and he slipped to the ground, fighting a darkness that threatened to engulf him. As the ground dipped crazily under him, he felt his clothes being pulled back onto his frame by the barber and his wife. Through slitted eyes he watched as the barber slipped Longarm's wallet from his inside pocket. Longarm saw the hangman's list come out with it, but all the lines were down and there was nothing he could say or do. Slipping the wallet to his wife, the barber crumpled the list and flung it aside, then continued to dress him while his wife struggled to push on his boots. He groaned inwardly. He needed that list or more men would die, but when he tried to shake himself back to life, the kid—a grin on his face—rapped him smartly on the side of the head with his sap.

An indeterminate time later, Longarm felt himself being dragged through the gathering dusk into the back of the livery stable, after which he was flung facedown onto a horse's warm rump. The two men flung a rope under the horse and tied his ankles to his wrists. As they tightened the loop, Longarm's belly was yanked down hard onto the slick hide. Still groggy, but infuriated by this wholly unwarranted attack on him, Longarm cried out and struggled to free himself, wondering all the while where in hell the owner of the stable was.

The thin-faced pale one in the slicker came around the horse and grabbed a pile of Longarm's hair and lifted his head off the horse until they were eye to eye.

"Listen, you silly bastard," the kid said, tapping the side of Longarm's skull with the business end of his sap, "you want another go 'round with this?"

Aware of how sensitive his head had become of late, Longarm quieted at once. The kid let Longarm's face drop back down onto the horse's rump, and a moment later the two men mounted up and led his horse out of the livery into the gathering dusk. Before long they were out of town, following a trace that kept close alongside a stream.

Longarm was spectacularly uncomfortable: his brains threatened to come unstuck each time the horse planted a hoof, and its rolling gait threatened to slide him under its belly, until Longarm found a way to dig his knees into the animal's side. When he finally glanced back at

Red Bank, the town's gas-lit streets were already dropping below the horse's rump.

Goddamn it! Who were these cockroaches, and where in hell were they taking him?

Sometime past midnight, the full moon overhead as bright as a silver dollar, his horse carried him through a gate with the words Circle D painted in whitewashed letters across a crude arch fashioned from an old singletree. A half mile farther on, inside a ranch compound, he was cut loose and dumped to the ground in front of a horse barn, then dragged past the horses stamping in their stalls into a storeroom in back. The one called Gulch lit a lantern while his companion propped Longarm up against a wall.

The barber had evidently left Longarm's watch for the kid, who now lifted it from his vest pocket to examine it, the derringer attached to it by the gold-washed chain coming out with it. The kid examined the watch, then the belly gun, and decided to keep both. Meanwhile, Gulch was trying on Longarm's cross-draw rig. He found his belly too ample to make use of it, however, and flung it into a corner, contenting himself with sticking Longarm's .44 into his belt.

"You two mind telling me what this is all about?" Longarm asked.

"We're the ones askin' the questions," Gulch said, his big Colt cocked and ready as he leaned close over Longarm.

"You got questions, ask them."

"You're a stranger in town. Right?"

"Since when is that a crime?"

The kid, a trace of a smile on his thin face, stepped closer and kicked Longarm viciously in the ribs. He waited for Longarm to recover from it. Then he kicked Longarm again.

"For you, mister," the kid rasped softly, "maybe it is."

"Where you from?" asked Gulch.

The beginnings of an explanation for all this only now occurred to Longarm. "Wait a minute," he said patiently. "Just hold off and wait a minute. Looks like you two assholes've got me mixed up with someone else."

"That so?" Gulch said.

"Yeah. So put down that gun."

"Sure. I'll put it down." Gulch smashed the barrel across Longarm's face.

Longarm felt the blood flowing out of his left nostril and told himself not to lose his temper—not yet, anyway. "Hold off, you two!" he croaked. "I'm a U.S. deputy marshal. A federal officer."

"Hear that?" said the kid, grinning at Gulch. 'He's a federal marshal."

"Where's your badge?"

"In my wallet."

"Show us."

"The wallet's gone. The barber stole it."

"You expect us to believe that?"

"I think you'd better," Longarm told them, wiping

away the steady flow of blood seeping into his mouth. "Before you hit me again."

"All right, mister," said Gulch, "suppose you tell me what you're doin' in this territory?"

"I'm after Johnny Danfield."

"And who the hell is he?"

Longarm sighed. It was useless. Obviously, these two maniacs had been sent to town to pick up any suspicious-looking strangers. But no one, obviously, had bothered to tell them why.

"Look," Longarm said reasonably. "You two can still save your asses if you let me see your boss. Go on in now and wake him up. I'll talk to him and nobody else."

"There's already been too much talk," the kid told Gulch, pulling the sap out of his pocket. He looked at Gulch. "Let's get some shut-eye. We can deliver this here marshal to Frank in the morning."

The kid moved closer and swung the sap. Longarm held up his arm and tried to duck aside, but the sap caught him in the ribs and flung him back against the wall. Crunched against it, he slipped into a weak, foggy state and was unable to fight back as they bound his wrists and ankles behind him with strips of rawhide. They left the storeroom and Longarm heard the bolt on the door ram home, followed by the sound of their heavy boots tramping out of the barn.

He leaned his head back wearily.

It was all a damn fool mistake. He had more than likely found the man he had come to warn—or more accurately, two of his not very bright ranch hands had found *him*. Inching himself back against a nail he discovered sticking out of the wall, he began thrusting the rawhide against its sharp point.

Chapter 8

Taylor stirred. It seemed to him that he had slept enough. The pain in his belly had receded to a small, persistent ache. If the tiny ravening beast in there was not dead, at least it was dozing. He sat up. The room's corners yawned open like the mouths of canyons at midnight. The two windows were lopsided, and then he understood. He was still asleep, back inside one of his drugged nightmares.

Or was he?

Scratching his head, he stood up and tottered over to the window and gazed down at the street below. It was not yet dark, but the street's gas lamps were lit already, shedding a fitful glow over the main street and turning the storefronts just under them into gaping mouths. Three saloons were visible from his window, all running wide open. From where he stood, Taylor could hear clearly the harsh bark of male laughter together with the clumsy, shuffling stomp of their boots in time with the piano's jaunty, tinkling beat. One saloon down the street boasted a cornet player, his high, trilling melody cutting through the dusk.

Down the sidewalk ran a barefoot kid in a straw hat and bib overalls, slapping at a metal hoop to keep it going. Wobbling crazily, the hoop surged along, occasionally bounding over breaks in the wooden sidewalk. So concentrated on the hoop was the boy, he nearly ran down two ladies of the night, who were forced to dart into the street to avoid him. As he slapped the hoop on past them, hardly aware of their presence, they shook their parasols at him and shrilled obscenities; then they returned to the sidewalk and pushed through the batwings of the saloon directly across from the hotel.

His head was clearing, Taylor realized. The opium induced distortions were fading. And maybe the tiny, gnawing rodent in his gut was coming alive as well. He was about to return to his bed for another swig of laudanum when he saw something that made him think he might possibly be seeing things again.

Longarm, his long frame draped over the back of a horse, was being led from the livery stable by two riders he had never seen before. There was no doubt it was Longarm because his face was turned toward the hotel as he passed under a street lamp, and there was no mistaking the lawman's chiseled, Indian-like features. Hatless, his tobacco-colored hair was shaggy and unkempt, this despite the fact that Longarm had left hours ago to get a haircut as well as a bath and shave.

Bolting from the window, Taylor pulled on his boots,

dressed and left his room, buckling on his gun belt as he descended the stairs to the hotel lobby. In the time it took for him to reach the street, dusk had fallen and the two riders were barely visible as they rode out of town. Taylor did not have a horse saddled, so he could not mount up and overtake them on the instant. He comforted himself with the knowledge that he still had plenty of time, since the riders were sticking to the road and were not pushing their mounts.

His reaction was slow, his thoughts like heavy boots stepping through tar, a residue of the opium still in his brain. He shook his head and tried to concentrate. Maybe he should take the first horse he found at a hitch rack and ride out after them two.

No. That was crazy. First things first, he told himself. He had to find out what had happened, then saddle up and ride after Longarm.

Energized now, he crossed the street to the barbershop and found it closed. He ducked into the alley and came out behind it, pushing through the gate leading into the fenced-in bathing area. Skirting an overturned wooden bathtub, he saw Longarm's hat lying in a corner. He hurried over and picked it up. As he did so, his eye caught sight of a crumpled piece of paper. Tucking Longarm's hat under his arm, he flattened out the piece of paper and, squinting in the dim light, was able to make out the names on the hangman's list Longarm had been carrying.

Refolding and pocketing the list, he dropped Longarm's hat beside the barbershop's back door, tried the knob and found the door unlocked. Pushing it open, he stepped inside the building and closed the door softly behind him. He was in a narrow hallway. At its far end, a door leading into the kitchen was partially open. The room was lit brightly and from inside it came the voice of a man arguing querulously with a woman.

He walked lightly down the hall, the sound of his progress masked by the upraised voices. When he was able to see fully into the kitchen, he held up. In the middle of the kitchen table Longarm's wallet lay open, and beside it were his bank notes. Sitting at the table, Taylor saw what he assumed was the barber and his Indian wife. The barber was a swollen bag of suet with the pale, soft fingers of a woman. His wife was already in her nightgown, two long strands of braided hair hanging down her back.

Taylor stepped boldly into the kitchen.

The barber jumped up so hastily he overturned his chair. His wife remained seated, but her hand dropped under her gown, reappearing instantly with a bone-handled skinning knife.

"Here, you!" the barber said. "How'd you get in here?"

"You blind? I walked in."

"I'm closed for the day. You'll have to come back tomorrow."

"Don't want a shave or a haircut, or a bath."

"Well, goddamn it, what *do* you want?"

Taylor lifted his Navy Colt from its holster and leveled the muzzle on the barber. "Where'd you get that wallet?"

The Indian woman surged out of her chair. As she slashed down at him with her knife, he ducked hastily aside, then struck the woman with his gun barrel, catching her on the side of her head. The force of his blow was enough to send her reeling back against her chair. Her knees folded and she toppled backward, the knife clattering to the kitchen floor.

Taylor picked up the knife and stuck it into his belt, then leveled his six-gun on the barber, who was looking in some amazement at his wife crumpled on the floor—as if this were the first time he had ever seen her bested.

Turning to Taylor, the barber shrugged. "All right. All right. Take the wallet. I don't want it."

"And the money."

"That too. I won't argue. You got the gun."

"Tell me how you got the wallet."

"Found it outside, near one of my tubs. Someone must've dropped it."

"While he was being assaulted?"

"All right. So there was a fight."

"And when you got the chance you lifted the wallet."

The barber swallowed, then shrugged hopelessly, his eyes on the Navy Colt's muzzle. "How the hell was I supposed to know he was a federal marshal."

"Where's his badge?"

He indicated his wife on the floor behind the overturned chair with a quick nod of his head. "She got rid

143

of it. She knew it'd do us no good to get caught with a lawman's badge."

"Where are those two men taking the marshal?"

Eager to cooperate now, frantic to exculpate himself, the barber told Taylor the two men were taking Longarm to the Circle D.

"Why would they want to take him out there?"

"Because they're on the prod, came into town looking for any suspicious strangers. And that tall lawman sure filled the bill."

"Who owns the Circle D?"

"Frank Dannenhower."

Jesus, Taylor thought. Longarm had been sure he'd have no trouble, once they reached Red Bank, finding Frank Dannenhower. But it sure as hell hadn't occurred to him that Dannenhower and his men would be out looking for him.

"Where's his spread?"

"A three, four hour ride from here."

"That the best you can do?"

"Hell, I never been out there."

The barber's wife, her hands clasping the overturned chair, was slowly pulling herself up off the kitchen floor, her eyes, bright with malevolence, riveted on Taylor. Perfectly well aware that she might launch herself at him a second time, Taylor aimed the Colt at her throat and cocked the hammer. The sound it made echoed loudly in the small kitchen.

"Tell your hellcat to get back down on the floor,"

Taylor told the barber, "or you'll be sleeping in an empty bed tonight."

The barber told her to stay where she was, and like a whipped cat, she settled back down behind the chair, her fierce eyes never leaving Taylor's. He quickly stepped over to the table, stuffed Longarm's bank notes into his wallet, then backed out of the kitchen. Turning, he ran lightly down the hallway and out of the building.

Sweeping up Longarm's hat, he hurried down the alley to the rear of the livery stable and ducked inside. He was looking for his roan when the hostler appeared with a shotgun in his hands. The old man looked quite unhappy, and there was a good reason for it. Apparently someone had just recently used his face to sharpen a gun barrel.

"Where's my horse?" Taylor asked.

"The roan?"

"Yes."

"Over here."

Limping noticeably, the old man led Taylor to a stall where Taylor saw that the roan's left front foreleg was wrapped in a bandage. The old man ducked into the stall and lifted the leg. "Lookee here," he said, "see how this leg's all swolled up? You mean you didn't notice that when you rode in?"

"No, I didn't. She wasn't limping then."

" 'Spose that's possible," the hostler allowed grudgingly. "Just noticed the swelling myself an hour ago."

"I still need a horse."

"How long you want it for?"

"Long enough for me to ride out to the Circle D."

The old man pulled up to stare at Taylor. "Them cocksuckers? Now why in hell you want to have anything to do with them?"

"They've taken a friend of mine out there. From the look of it, against his will."

"Jesus. So that's why they clobbered me, them bastards. They also took my best packhorse without payin'. They're getting so they think they're the only law there is around here."

Taylor leaned close to inspect the old man's face. "Looks like they banged you up pretty bad. If I had time, maybe I could fix it some. I'm a doctor."

"It was the kid with Gulch who done it. He likes to use that sap of his. He got off the train from the East three months ago and this here country ain't been the same since. He's pure meanness."

"How do I get out to the Circle D?"

"Follow the stream out of town. When you come to the canyon, cut due south. Just keep on the trace till you run into the hills. Then keep going. You can't miss it."

"I still need that horse," Taylor reminded him patiently.

"Follow me. I just bought me a fine animal."

The hostler led him into the rear of the stable, pausing in front of a stall containing a handsome, powerful black. It looked a mite strung out, as if it had been ridden hard and far.

And it was a black.

Taylor turned to the hostler. "You say you just bought this horse?"

"Yep, and fer a damn good price."

"Who sold it to you?"

"Jim Tucker of the Lazy J. He left town on the stage. That man sure was in a hurry. Owes most everyone in town, including Frank Dannenhower. Lousiest card player I ever did see."

"Whereabouts is the Lazy J ranch?"

"It runs alongside the Circle D, clear to the foothills. You want this horse, or don't you?"

"How much?"

"Three dollars a day."

"That's pretty steep, ain't it? Make it two."

"Done. But I'll be wanting a day in advance."

Taylor counted the money out into the old man's palm, then returned to the hotel. He dropped Longarm's wallet and hat on his bed and slipped his last bottle of laudanum from his bedroll. Hurrying back to the stable, he saddled the big black and rode out of town, following the stream. The horse appeared strung out when he first mounted it, but its brief residence in the stable had made him feisty and filled him with gas. He farted and pranced outrageously, and Taylor did not find him easy to handle.

By the time he reached the canyon and cut south to the Circle D, he was completely drained, with not a single spark of energy left. Meanwhile, the gnawing beast inside his gut had awakened from its slumber, its teeth sharp and getting sharper by the minute. Unable to ignore his growing discomfort and weary from fighting what he could not control, a few miles south of the canyon he reined in the black and slid wearily from the saddle.

In a sudden, perspiring fever of urgency, he pulled the bottle of laudanum from his saddlebag, unstoppered it, and gulped down the dark liquid. He caught himself before he emptied the bottle, tethered the black to a sapling and slumped to the ground, telling himself he would off-saddle the horse later. His back resting against a boulder, he tipped the bottle up a second time, drank greedily, then pulled the bottle down with trembling hands, fearful that he might drain the bottle's contents.

This was his last bottle.

And he did not know where he would get another.

Stoppering the bottle, he laid it beside him on the grass, as carefully as a mother would her babe. The alcohol and opium mixture had already struck his stomach with an explosive force, its furry warmth reaching out through his limbs and surging into his skull.

As its sweet, numbing warmth transformed him, he glanced up and saw a dancing moon and huge alley cats coming out of the night to join him, their feline tails twitching, their yellow eyes gleaming in the night. Purring, they prowled closer, nudging him seductively; he felt their hot breath on his face; then a sudden, unreasonable panic filled him and he tried to push away the closest cat, only to find it was no longer a cat but the barber's Indian wife. Before he could protect himself, she towered over him, then plunged her dagger into his stomach. He doubled up, crying out—realized dimly what he was experiencing was only the opium, and spun off finally into the oblivion he craved.

When he awoke the next morning, the gnawing in his gut was still there, faint, dim, persistent. As always when he awoke to steady pain, he felt a nearly overpowering sense of futility and despair, for it impressed on him as nothing else did the hopelessness of his condition, and the terrible, inevitable course his malignancy was taking.

He sat up. His mouth was so dry he found it painful to swallow, and though he was hungry, the moment he thought of food his stomach heaved in protest, and he almost got sick. He unstoppered the bottle and downed the rest of the laudanum, then flung the bottle aside and got shakily to his feet. He had not taken his saddle off the horse overnight and felt genuinely bad about that as he untied the black and mounted up.

The bright, milky sky caused him to squint as he peered ahead, but it was as if his lids no longer had the ability to shield his eyes from the sun. He pulled his hat brim down further and kept on south. What remained of the laudanum in his system caused his thoughts to crawl like slugs over a sinkhole; consecutive, logical thought seemed impossible. What he judged to be an hour later, he found himself riding through tall, lush grasslands containing clumps of the Circle D's heavily larded beef cattle.

He was getting close.

Cresting a rise, he saw three riders about a hundred

yards distant watching him from a ridge. One of them was peering at him through a pair of binoculars. Taylor didn't like the feel of it, especially when he considered how badly Longarm had been used by this outfit.

He kept on without pause and was in the swale below the ridge when they swept down off the crest, surrounding him so swiftly his head spun. The three riders regarded him with undisguised hostility.

"What're you doin' on my land?" one of them demanded.

"You Frank Dannenhower?"

"Jesus, Frank," said one of the other two riders, a stout fellow with a round, baby face. "He knows you. Do you know him?"

"No, I don't," said Frank, drawing his six-gun.

"Search him," said the taller of the three.

Taylor tried to pull his horse back, but Dannenhower leaned over and swept Taylor off his horse with one vicious swipe of his six-gun. Groggy from the blow, his senses spinning, Taylor remained where he had fallen as the other two riders flung themselves from their mounts and rifled his pockets. It was the tall, stringy one who pulled from his pocket the hangman's list Taylor had found in back of the barbershop. Until that moment he had forgotten that he had kept it.

Pushing himself upright, he tried to snatch back the list. But the man who had taken it ducked back easily, lifting the paper so he could read the names.

"My God, look here, Frank," he said. "Your name's

on this here list, sixth from the bottom. And there's Wade's name and Rog's . . . and Nat.''

"Look here," demanded Taylor. "I can explain that."

The short, baby-faced one slipped Taylor's Navy Colt from his holster while Frank Dannenhower took the hangman's list and read it himself. Finished, he folded the list and put it in his pocket, his face like a piece of granite, his eyes as hard as nails.

"Well, well, well. You rode right into our lap. You're the son of a bitch we been waitin' for."

"You're wrong," protested Taylor. "I'm not the one who's after you."

"You ain't?"

"No! It's not me you want, it's Johnny Danfield."

"Johnny Danfield?"

"Yes. He's the one you want, and I'm not him."

" 'Course you won't admit who you are."

The chunky one broke in. "You're ridin' a black, ain't you?"

"I can explain that. This ain't my horse."

The little man snorted derisively.

"And who else but the hangman," Frank Dannenhower broke in, "would make a list of every damn member of that posse?"

"That's not my list!"

"I see. That ain't your horse—and this ain't your list."

Frank Dannenhower looked from one man to the other, a thin, derisive smile on his face.

"I know how it looks," Taylor said, "but just give me a chance to explain."

"Explain this, you bastard."

Dannenhower lifted his gun and fired. The round caught Taylor in the right chest, spinning him completely around. Somehow, he remained on his feet and started to run. Then the other two opened up on him. The spray of slugs plowed into his back with enough force to propel him violently forward. He lost his balance and sprawled facedown in the grass. He tried to move, but was unable to do so. He was enough of a physician to know that their bullets had severed his spinal cord.

He thought he heard approaching hoofbeats and above them someone's cry; for a crazy instant he imagined it was Longarm. An explosion of gunfire followed, but he was unable to turn his head and too tired to pay it any heed. Besides, it did not seem to matter. Nothing mattered. Everything in the universe had come to a pause, and he knew now what it meant for time to stand still. The pain was gone. He became aware of a great calm falling over him, and in that moment knew he could not hate his three killers. In shooting him down like this, they had delivered him from a miserable, fruitless existence, and from a death too terrible to contemplate.

Even so, he was sorry he didn't reach Longarm. He wanted to tell him where to find Johnny Danfield.

Chapter 9

Two hours earlier that same morning, Longarm had managed to break out of his tiny prison.

Struggling all night, he had finally been able to pull the remaining strands of rawhide off his bloodied wrists, then untie his ankles. At once he tried to break out of the storeroom. He flung his shoulder against the door, but found it solid. Each time he hit it, he could hear the hasp grating against the lock. But it did not give an inch. He kicked the door a couple of times, to no avail. He thought of shouting through the door for help, but he didn't know for sure what he was up against on this spread and wasn't all that eager to renew acquaintance with Gulch and the kid.

Deciding finally that his wisest course would be to wait for the return of the two who had put him there, he probed about in the pitch-black gloom for something to use as a club. His fingers closed at last about a sawed-off two-by-four partially hidden under a pile of grain sacks. He was hefting the four-foot-long piece of lumber in order to find the most secure grip when he heard footsteps approaching.

He crouched in the storeroom's farthest corner as someone slid the bolt aside and flung open the door. The one called Gulch entered, the kid following close behind him. The solid gloom was only partially penetrated by the dim light that entered with them, and Longarm saw Gulch frowning as he peered into the corner where he had left Longarm. Waiting until both men were inside, Longarm flung himself out of the corner and charged into them, his two-by-four slamming into Gulch's right side with bone-crunching force. Then he clobbered Gulch repeatedly about the head and shoulders, driving him back into the kid. As Gulch sagged to the floor, leaving the kid unprotected, Longarm swung hard, catching the kid in the neck with a brutal rabbit punch—a sort of return favor. The kid slumped to the floor, barely conscious.

Longarm flung aside the two-by-four and reached into the kid's slicker for his blackjack. As he withdrew the sap, the kid blinked dazedly up at him, one hand upraised as it pawed the air feebly. Longarm planted his feet and swung the sap. The weighted end crunched into the kid's left cheekbone, shattering it. The kid flipped over and lay perfectly still beside his partner.

Bending over them, Longarm found they were still breathing. It would not have pained him if they had not been. After slipping his .44 from Gulch's belt, he recovered his watch and derringer from a deep inside

154

pocket in the kid's slicker. His cross-draw rig was still in the corner where Gulch had flung it. He buckled it back on, slipped his .44 into it, then draped his watch chain once more across his vest, somewhat annoyed to find that his vest had lost two buttons. Missing only his wallet and hat, Longarm strode from the storeroom, closed the door behind him and slid the bolt. Taking his time, he searched out a suitable mount and a saddle to go with it.

Once he found what he wanted, he saddled the horse, mounted up, and ducking his head, rode out of the barn, past a few puzzled ranch hands bent over the water trough in front of the bunkhouse, towels draped over their necks.

Dismounting before the main ranch house, Longarm dropped his reins over the hitch rack as a tall Indian woman stepped out onto the porch.

"I'm looking for Frank Dannenhower, ma'am," he told her.

"He already left," she said.

"Would you happen to know where to?"

A grizzled old cowhand strolled over. He was carrying his straight razor and one side of his face was still lathered.

"I saw them ride out, mister," he said as the Indian woman ducked back into the house. He wore a small hat with curled brims, patched Levi's, and a faded red-checked cotton shirt, unbuttoned down the front now since he was in the midst of his morning toilet.

"That warn't the boss's missus," he explained to

155

Longarm. "She's just his Injin housekeeper—and mebbe a little else besides."

"I guessed that."

"Didn't I just see you ride out of the horse barn?"

"I got here late last night and slept in there. Didn't want to wake anyone in the bunkhouse."

"That was right decent of you. Where's your hat?"

"Lost it."

"I got one you can borrow. It never fit me, but it looks like your size."

"I'd sure appreciate it."

"You looking for a job?"

"This a good ranch to work, is it?"

"Grub's good, but Dannenhower's a mean one. Just stay out of his way, if you can—him and the foreman."

"You say Mr. Dannenhower just rode out?"

"Yep. Him and his two guests. They're headin' into town, carrying enough artillery to start a war. A jumpy bunch, lately, the three of 'em. Wish I knew what they was so all-fired nervous about."

Longarm swung into his saddle, hoping the old-timer would not notice the Circle D brand it wore.

"You headin' after them?" the old-timer asked, squinting up at Longarm.

Longarm nodded.

"You could stay here and wait for them to get back. Cookie's got fresh coffee on, an' he won't mind another hand at the table."

"Thanks, but I want to see Mr. Dannenhower."

"I'll go get that hat."

Longarm watched the old, bandy-legged cowpoke hurry back to the bunkhouse, feeling a mite uncomfortable about taking advantage of his generosity. Still, he had no choice in the matter. The old-timer returned with a tan Stetson and handed it up to him. It was pretty battered and needed a cleaning, but it fit well enough and would serve to keep the sun off.

"Much obliged," Longarm said.

"You don't have to return it. If it fits, you can keep it."

Longarm thanked the old cowpoke again, swung his horse about and cantered across the yard, following the rutted trace. As soon as he was out of sight of the ranch buildings, he lifted his horse to a steady, ground-devouring lope. It turned out he had chosen well. This Circle D horse's stride was steady and powerful, and it was eager to run.

Sooner than he expected, Longarm came upon three riders sitting their mounts on the crest of a ridge a good half mile ahead of him. Between Longarm and the crest extended a long, grassy swale—with Circle D beef partially hidden in the grass like bugs in pea soup. Bugs with horns.

He clapped spurs to his mount and was halfway to the ridge when the three riders charged off down it and disappeared. Longarm kept on, crested the ridge and saw Dannenhower and his two companions on a flat below crowding around Doc Taylor.

Jesus Christ! What the hell was the doc doing out here?

Groaning, sensing bad trouble, Longarm booted his horse off the ridge toward the small knot of men. Before he reached them, however, one of the men lifted his side arm and pumped a shot into the doc. The force of the slug spun the doc around, and then he began to run. Furious, Longarm drew his .44 and cried out a warning to the three men, telling them to hold off; but his cry was lost in the murderous flurry of gunfire that punched holes into the doc's back, driving him forward and to the ground.

From the way Taylor was sprawled, Longarm knew he was dead or close to it. Still screaming at the men, Longarm flung up his .44 and began firing. Apparently unaware of him until that moment, the three men leaped astride their horses and charged back up the slope. Icy cold with fury, Longarm pulled up, tracked the last rider and squeezed off a shot. The rider flung up his arms and tumbled backward off his horse.

The other two riders vanished beyond the crest of the ridge. Longarm yanked his horse around and spurred over to where the doc lay. Dismounting, he leaned close to the doc.

"Doc! It's me. Longarm! How bad you hurt?"

For a moment there was no response. Then Longarm found himself looking into the doc's smiling face. He looked foolishly happy.

"I'm hurt bad enough," he answered, "bad enough to take me out of all this shit."

"Jesus. Don't say that."

"Why not? It is the truth. And I am most grateful.

You remember, don't you, what God had in mind for me earlier.''

"What the hell happened here?"

"My fault . . . rode a black . . . then let them find that hangman's list on me."

"You had the list?"

"Picked it up . . . behind the barbershop."

"Who was that bastard, the one who shot you first?"

"Frank Dannenhower. . . ."

"Jesus! The man we rode all this way to warn?"

"Remarkable, isn't it." ·

Longarm sat back on his heels, hating this. Remembering his earlier dismissal of the doc as an addict did not help at all. Since joining him, the doc had given up whiskey and had kept himself reasonably clean, not an easy task on the trail. During the long days and nights they had spent on the trail since leaving the horse ranch, Longarm had come to like the physician and to understand his grim struggle—one he was waging without self-pity or a single word of complaint.

"I don't have . . . much time," the doc whispered. "Lean closer, I got something to tell you."

"What is it?"

"I know where Johnny Danfield is."

"Where?"

"The Lazy J ranch. It's around here, somewhere."

"How do you know this?"

The doc's lidded eyes flicked to the big black, indifferently cropping the lush grass at its feet.

"That's where . . . the black came from."

"I'll check it out."

". . . careful . . ."

"Yeah."

"I'll sleep . . . now."

"Sure."

The doc closed his eyes. Longarm got up and looked away with stinging eyes, cursing silently, bitterly. It wasn't at all difficult now for Longarm to understand what had happened ten years earlier when those posse members strung up an innocent man and made an orphan of his son.

Longarm found himself wondering which man he wanted most at that moment—Johnny Danfield or Frank Dannenhower.

Chapter 10

With some reluctance Longarm walked over to the rider
he had brought down. The man had not moved after
striking the ground and Longarm had assumed he was
beyond help. He hunkered down beside the quiet body
and found himself gazing at a chunky fellow with a
pudgy, babyish face. Longarm rolled him over. The
bullet had cracked his spine and from the surprised look
on his face, Longarm was pretty certain he had died
instantly.

Tying both corpses over their horses, Longarm brought
them back to Red Bank and left them with an unhappy
undertaker demanding to know who would pay for their
burials. Ignoring him, Longarm crossed to his hotel and
browbeat the desk clerk into giving him the key to Doc
Taylor's room.

Inside it, as he was collecting the doc's personal
gear, he was surprised and pleased to find that Taylor
had recovered his hat and wallet and thrown them onto

the bed. The doc must have paid a visit to the barber-shop, Longarm realized. Opening the wallet, he saw his bank notes tucked into the fold; but his badge was missing. He had a pretty good idea where to find that, however; and clapping on his hat, he left the hotel and crossed the street to the barbershop.

The barber, straight razor in hand, was bent over a lathered face, his razor scratching steadily as he pulled the blade up past the Adam's apple toward the chin line. At sight of Longarm, the barber went as pale as the lather on the customer's face.

"Put down the razor, Mac," said Longarm, smiling coldly. "You might cut the man's throat."

"What do you want?"

"I want my badge back."

"My wife . . . she got rid of it."

"Go back in there, Mac, and convince her to find it."

The barber put down the razor and hurried through the curtained doorway leading to his living quarters. A heated, shrill disputation arose at once, the barber's deeper voice growing in volume with each passing moment, the woman's eerie, shrieking rejoinders caus-ing Longarm to grimace. The customer in the barber chair flung off his sheet and fled out the door.

A chair went over and someone landed heavily. An awesome silence followed. A moment later the barber, a knife wound opening one cheek, appeared in the doorway, Longarm's badge in his hand.

"Here it is," he said, handing it to Longarm. "I don't know why the hell she wanted to keep it."

"For a trophy. You know, like a scalp."

The barber shuddered.

"You better see to that cut on your face."

He glanced over his shoulder, then leaned closer to Longarm. "You should see her. This time I think I might've killed her."

"You're not that lucky."

Longarm fitted the badge into his wallet and left the shop, then went in search of Tad Duncan, the county sheriff. It had not gone unnoticed that a stranger had led two dead men into town slung over the backs of their horses. The sheriff was on the porch of his jailhouse, leaning against a porch post, his arms folded over his chest.

Longarm halted in front of the porch. "Howdy, Sheriff."

"You the gent just brought in two dead men?"

"I'll tell you all about it, but inside, not out here."

The sheriff turned and disappeared into his office. Longarm mounted the porch steps and followed in after him. The two men introduced themselves. When Longarm found he was all out of cheroots, the sheriff produced a cigar, which, under the circumstances, Longarm found himself perfectly willing to accept.

Striding behind his desk, the sheriff slacked into his swivel chair, leaned back and watched Longarm light up. Duncan was almost Longarm's height, with snow-white hair and mustache. His blue eyes were sharp and at the moment they watched Longarm with a keen curiosity.

"All right, Long. You want to tell me about them two bodies?"

"One of them was a man I deputized. Dr. Cyrus Taylor, late of Sand Creek, Wyoming Territory. The other one I never laid eyes on before I shot him."

"*You* shot him?"

"A few minutes after he shot my deputy."

"Maybe you better start at the beginning."

Longarm began with his and Doc Taylor's reason for coming to Red Bank in the first place and went on from there, including his escape from Gulch and the kid, finishing up with an account of Doc Taylor's death.

Duncan sat up straight in his chair, a frown on his face. "I hear what you say, Long. And I believe you. But we still got a problem. If I ride out to the Circle D and haul Frank Dannenhower back here for shooting down your partner, he'll be out on bail in less'n ten minutes. And at the inquest, it'll be his word against yours. He'll most likely claim your man drew first."

"I know that."

"So what do you want me to do?"

"Nothing, for now. Later, I might need you to back my story. As one lawman to another."

"You ain't goin' after Frank yourself, are you?"

"Hell," Longarm said, getting to his feet. "Only a damn fool would take on a man as powerful as Frank Dannenhower." He turned and started from the office. "Good day, Sheriff."

As Longarm rode out of Red Bank less than an hour later, he was aware that the sheriff would more than likely telegraph Billy Vail to make sure Longarm was the man he said he was, which was precisely what Longarm hoped he would do. It would save Longarm the time it would have taken him to exchange telegrams with Vail, and it would tell Billy what he would need to know in the event Longarm came out of this on the short end.

The night before, Johnny thought he had seen smoke from a camp fire somewhere in the timber above the ranch house, and this morning he had decided to investigate. He had found nothing, however, and was breaking out of the timbered slope on foot when he caught sight of the Navaho galloping into the compound below him. Jumping off his pinto, the Indian ducked into the barn, and a moment later he and Jess hurried out of the back of the barn and halted on a rise. Shading her eyes, Jess peered down the long slope at a distant meadow far below. Following her gaze, Johnny saw through a gap in the trees two riders approaching.

Johnny kept on down the slope toward Jess and the Navaho. His second day out of bed, he was still a bit weak in the knees; but he was on his feet now and no longer in much pain, though he could not yet take a really deep breath. He figured he would know a lot more about his true condition when he stepped into a saddle once again.

Jess saw him coming and hurried over. "I didn't see you go out, Johnny. How do you feel?"

"I'm okay. Looks like you got visitors."

"This is not a social call, Johnny."

"Who are they?"

"Harry Gulch, the Circle D foreman, and someone they call the kid. Everyone seems to be afraid of him. He's from the East."

"And you figure they're trouble?"

She nodded grimly. "When the kid and Gulch show up, most people around here keep an eye on their silverware."

"What do they want?"

"My ranch."

"Maybe you better explain that."

"When Jim married me, he figured that gave him equal rights to the Lazy J. He was wrong, but he wouldn't let me tell him any different. Last week, to cover a bet, he signed over the Lazy J's deed to the owner of the Circle D."

"Who owns the Circle D?"

"Frank Dannenhower."

Johnny recognized the name at once. It came as something of a shock to find himself this close to the man he had come so far to find, but he managed to keep his composure. Looking past the Navaho at the oncoming riders, he realized they were still a good distance away.

"Why does this cattleman want your place, Jess?"

"His land borders mine. Lazy J land would give him access to more water. He could double his herd size."

"You don't have to give him anything, not if the land's yours."

"He knows that. I know that." She shook her head ruefully. "But that won't stop Frank Dannenhower."

"Let him take it out of Jim's hide then."

"Jim's gone, Johnny. He lit out. Took the stage three days ago."

"I looked for my horse this morning. He's the one took it?"

She nodded unhappily. "I was going to tell you. He sold it for the price of his ticket. A couple of days ago, Juan went into town for some provisions and found out the owner of the livery stable bought it."

"It don't matter. I'll get it later."

He looked down the slope at the approaching riders. He could see their faces clearly now. "We better get back to the ranch house, Jess, to set up a reception for these two."

"I don't want any violence, Johnny."

"We look strong enough, there won't be any."

Johnny waved to Juan, and the three of them turned and cut back through the barn.

Less than five minutes later, rifle in hand, Johnny eased himself flat on the floor of the barn's hayloft as the two riders pulled up in front of the ranch house. In the clump of cottonwoods on the other side of the house, Johnny knew, the Navaho was crouching with his own rifle.

Johnny was not impressed by Dannenhower's foreman, the one she called Gulch. He looked to be a real slob. Troublesome, maybe, but not very clever. The young kid in the gray slicker and derby hat, however,

167

looked mean enough to be dangerous. Both men had been torn up some not too long ago. Gulch had ridden up favoring his right side, like a man with cracked ribs, and there was a purplish welt on the kid's right cheekbone, the eye above it swollen nearly shut.

Jess appeared in the ranch house doorway toting a rifle. When Johnny had protested her intention to do this, she had convinced him she knew how to use the rifle, insisting she'd been shooting game with it since she was seven years old.

Gulch shifted his weight on his saddle. "No need for that rifle, Jess."

"Speak your piece and ride out."

"That ain't very friendly, Jess."

Lifting the muzzle of her rifle, Jess said, "I don't intend to be friendly, Gulch. Not to the likes of you."

"Frank wants Jim. He owes Frank."

Jess lowered the rifle some. "Jim's gone. I'm surprised you didn't know."

"Gone? Where?"

"I don't know, and I don't care. He talked a lot about California, if that helps any."

"He's a welcher, Jess. He ain't got no right to run out like that."

"Just the same, he did. And good riddance."

"I hate to be the one to tell you, Jess. But in that case, Frank owns the Lazy J. Jim signed over the deed to him."

"It wasn't his deed to sign over."

"Maybe so, but Frank's got a good lawyer."

"He can bring on his lawyers if he wants. That don't scare me none. I can hire as many as he can."

The kid spoke up then, in a curiously scratchy voice. "Frank's a generous man, Jess. He's willin' to buy you out, and at a good price."

"I'm not selling at any price."

"Why not?" asked Gulch. "You ain't got no one except the Navaho to help you run this spread. You need a man around here, a real man."

"I'm not selling. And you can tell Frank that's final."

"Now, Jess," Gulch said, grinning, "you know you need a man around here to help out."

"Yeah," said the kid, "someone to show you who's boss."

Abruptly, both men dismounted, and ignoring the gun in Jess's hand, started toward her. They apparently had no fear at all that she would open up on them point-blank. Suddenly uncertain, Jess took a step back into the doorway.

Abruptly, both men drew their irons, turned their backs on Jess and opened up a withering fire on the bushes behind which the Navaho was crouching. Hit, the Indian jumped up, staggered into view, then collapsed. At the same time both men whirled and this time began spraying the barn loft. The bullets slammed through the barn's flimsy siding, punching out large splinters and whining past Johnny's head. He scuttled back away from the open hayloft door and heard the two men running into the barn beneath him.

"We know you're up there, Jim," Gulch cried.

"Come on down," called the kid. "We won't hurt you!"

Johnny didn't answer. He heard the two men moving about below him and was figuring how to get a clear shot at them when he heard a lantern smash against the side of the barn, followed by the sudden, explosive whoosh of flames. Black smoke began pumping up through the flooring. The bastards. They were going to burn him out—Jess, too. If she didn't have a place to live, she'd have no choice but to sell out to Dannenhower. Jess had been right. This was no social call.

He heard Jess's screams and hurried back to the front of the loft. Peering through a grimy window, he saw the kid holding Jess, one hand wrapped around her neck, the other reaching down the front of her dress. There was a lewd, happy grin on his face.

Gulch ran from the barn then and turned to look back at the loft. "Throw down your weapon, Jim, or you'll fry!"

"Let Jess go!" Johnny yelled above the roar of the flames.

"Throw down your rifle first!"

Johnny went to the loft door and flung out his weapon. "Get away from her!"

"Sure!" the kid cried. "Soon's we finish with her!"

Gulch raised his six-gun, and fanning rapidly began spraying the loft. Johnny ducked low and tried to return

Gulch's fire, but when the kid joined in, their fusillade drove him back.

Abruptly, from behind the barn came the crack of a rifle. Gulch spun to the ground, then got up and raced for his horse. Another rifle shot followed, this round exploding at the kid's feet. The kid bolted for his horse. Wounded severely, Gulch had trouble pulling himself into his saddle. A third shot sent the kid's hat flying as he leaped into his saddle and spurred out of the compound, paying no heed to Gulch, who slipped from his horse, calling out feebly to the kid as he did so. Without a single backward glace at Gulch, the kid rode off.

All of this Johnny saw from the loft. Behind him the flames were chewing up through the floor, blistering his hide. He had no choice but to jump to the ground below. He did, landing hard. Instantly he felt a terrible, searing pain explode in his chest. He could hardly breathe, and when he tried to get up to escape the fierce heat, he could manage only a few crooked strides before collapsing. Head reeling, his chest on fire, he felt Jess dragging him away from the blazing barn.

Chapter 11

Like a puppet master watching from high above the stage, Longarm watched from a distant, pine-studded knoll as the kid rode his lathered mount into the Circle D compound and dashed for the ranch house. Soon, buckling their gun belts on, the man Longarm recognized as Frank Dannenhower and the other one he had seen shoot down Doc Taylor stomped out onto the porch. Longarm waited no longer. It was clear the Lazy J was going to get another visit—and soon.

Pulling his mount around, he galloped back to the Lazy J. Dismounting in the trees well back of the barn's charred, still-smoking wreckage, he tethered his heaving horse to a sapling and darted as quietly as he could the remaining distance to the ranch house, entering it with gun drawn. His surprise was complete. Johnny Danfield was slumped wearily in a chair at the kitchen table, his face drawn and pale, a cup of steaming hot coffee sitting on the table before him; the woman was at the stove, her face turned to him, eyes wide in astonishment.

"Who are you?" she cried.

Ignoring her, his .44 trained on Johnny Danfield, Longarm skirted the table, lifted Danfield's Colt from its holster and stuck it into his belt.

It was Johnny Danfield who answered the woman's question. "He's a lawman, Jess. That's what I figure, anyway. He's been after me for a while now." He looked at Longarm. "You're the one put this bullet in my chest."

"Yeah, while you were kicking the shit out of me."

"How'd you find me?"

"It wasn't easy. A late friend of mine had a hunch. I been up in the hills behind the ranch, prowling around, hoping to spot you. Last night I dropped some green pine boughs on my camp fire, hoping the smoke would draw you out. Looks like it worked."

"Mind telling me your name, mister?"

"Custis Long. I'm a U.S. deputy marshal."

"This here's Jess," Danfield said, smiling crookedly. "She owns this spread."

"And I gather Frank Dannenhower wants it."

"Yes. It was his men burned the barn this morning. They thought Jess's husband was hiding up there."

"I know. I was here."

Jess said, "Then you're the one who—"

"Drove them off? Yes, but that's not important now," Longarm told her. "Dannenhower and his men are on their way here right now to finish the job. I suggest you

174

ride in to Red Bank while Danfield and I prepare a proper welcome for them.''

"You?'' said Danfield. "You and me take on Frank Dannenhower?''

Longarm shrugged. "I don't like Frank Dannenhower any more than you do.''

Johnny Danfield tipped his head warily as he regarded Longarm. "And you're going to let me have my weapon back?''

"When the time comes.''

Johnny Danfield turned to the woman. "He makes sense, Jess. Get your buggy out of the shed and ride to town.''

"And you might tell the sheriff what's up,'' Longarm suggested to her. "If he can get out here with a small posse to back our play, it might help.''

Jess swiftly untied her apron. "I'll leave at once.'' She paused at the door. "Johnny. Those two bodies out there. Will you take care of them, Juan especially?''

Johnny nodded.

She left and Longarm heard her light footsteps running across the yard. Standing by Juan's riddled body a moment later, Longarm watched her drive off in the buggy, her whip cracking. Then Longarm glanced around for a spot to bury Gulch and the Indian.

"Up there, maybe,'' Johnny suggested, pointing to a small rise behind the ranch house.

Longarm agreed. It was as good a spot as any.

A few minutes later, the hasty burials done, the two men stood back and leaned on their shovels while they contemplated the fresh mounds of dirt before them—a grim reminder of what might lay ahead.

The moment passed.

"Let's go," said Longarm. "We got some tree climbing to do."

The two slipped quickly down the knoll. Johnny Danfield, Longarm noted, was moving well enough, but it was clear to him that Danfield was in considerable pain.

Crouched down behind a charred section of the barn's wall, Longarm held his Winchester at the ready, a fresh cartridge already cranked into the firing chamber. Through a slit in the charred wall, he could see Johnny Danfield hunkered down in the bushes on the other side of the compound, waiting for Longarm's signal. Grasped in Longarm's left hand was a nearly invisible strand of wire that led up into the biggest of the cottonwood trees shading the compound.

Abruptly, the dim pound of hooves he had been hearing for the last few minutes increased in volume, and a storm of riders clattered past the charred barn and pulled up in front of the ranch house as Frank Dannenhower pumped two rounds into the sky, the detonations reverberating off the surrounding hills.

"All right, Jim—Jess!" he cried. "Come out of there!"

It was apparent that Dannenhower had no idea Jim had run out, or who it was that the kid and Gulch had opened up on in the barn loft.

The lean, leathery rider next to Dannenhower dismounted and started toward the ranch house, gun drawn.

"Get back here, Ned. You'll get your ass shot off."

"I don't think there's anyone in there," Ned called back as he hopped onto the porch and kicked the door open.

When no fusillade greeted him, Ned looked back at Dannenhower. "They've lit out!" Then he turned around and walked inside.

The riders surrounding Dannenhower glanced at him eagerly, waiting for his response. Relief showed on each man's face. Gulch's apparent death and the prospect of more bloodshed was not something they regarded lightly.

Frank looked over at the kid. "Get down there, kid, and check out the house. And tell that fool Ned to get back here. I don't trust that fourflusher, or his wife, either."

The kid dismounted and followed after Ned into the ranch house. A moment later, considerably relieved, the two men stepped back out onto the porch.

"He's right, boss," said the kid. "The place is empty."

"What's been taken?"

"Nothing."

"Nothing? Nothing at all?"

"Not a stick."

"Then they'll be back."

"Guess you're right," said Ned, glancing nervously about.

"So I say we finish what we started," Dannenhower snapped. "Burn down the house, the sheds, the bunkhouse. Everything. I don't want them two to have anything to come back to."

"My God, Frank," said Ned. "You sure you want to go this far? You'll have the law down on you."

"This is my business, Ned," Dannenhower replied arrogantly. "I do what I want in this territory. And there ain't no law to stand in my way."

With a shrug, Ned descended the porch stairs and walked back to his horse and mounted up again, the kid following. Registered on a few of the crew members' faces, Longarm saw concern and distaste at what Frank Dannenhower was proposing. But these men were in a minority. Most of the riders were in favor of the action: their eyes fairly gleamed in anticipation.

Longarm searched among the Circle D's riders for the friendly old gent who'd lent him his hat. When he was certain the old man was not with this bunch, he stood up in plain sight, his Winchester leveled on Dannenhower. His sudden appearance startled them all, taking them completely by surprise. Not one of them had thought to glance or ride over to investigate the possibility of anyone hiding in the barn's smoking remains.

"Pull your men out of here," Longarm told Dannenhower. "Send them back to the Circle D. But you stay. I'm a U.S. deputy marshal, and I'm bringing you in."

"Hell you are! What's the charge?"

"Murder."

Dannenhower almost laughed aloud at the absurdity of it. "And just who am I supposed to have murdered?"

"My deputy, Doc Taylor."

"Your what?"

"The man you took the hangman's list from, the man you thought was Johnny Danfield."

"Damn your eyes, mister! That *was* the hangman we shot. He had the list on him!"

Longarm shifted his rifle to steady it. "Ten years ago you strung up the wrong man. You acted without giving him a chance to explain. And now you've done it again."

"Look here, mister," Dannenhower snapped. "I recognize you now. You're the one rode down on us and shot Pete. Put down that rifle right now, or you're a dead man."

The rider sitting his horse beside Dannenhower, the one called Ned, casually drew his own six-gun. "You'll be dead anyway, mister, for killing Pete."

As he spoke, he swung up his gun. Longarm ducked back down behind the wall as the man fired and tugged on the wire. High in the cottonwood, four tin cans, each filled with a gallon of kerosene, tipped, spilling their contents down over Dannenhower and his riders. Johnny Danfield stood up and heaved a blazing torch into their midst. There was a sudden *whump* as the kerosene exploded into flames, instantly engulfing the riders.

The kid, his slicker blazing, rode screaming toward the barn, flames flickering about his head like an infernal halo. As he swept by, Longarm put him out of his misery with a well-placed shot to the head. His screaming stopped abruptly as his terrified mount, its mane on fire, swept him out of sight. Meanwhile, a few of the men were pitched headlong from their horses, while the bulk of them, screaming in terror as they used their hats to slap at the flames, swung their horses around and galloped back the way they had come.

Dannenhower and Ned, along with their horses, caught most of the kerosene on their shoulders and hat brims and were sent flying off their frenzied mounts. On the ground they staggered about slapping at the flames running up their legs. Longarm saw Dannenhower run frantically toward the ranch house, then stumble and fall as a wall of flames encircled him. Darting out from cover, Longarm dragged the man's smoking torso through the flames to safety.

At that moment he heard an angry cry from Johnny Danfield and, glancing up, saw Johnny grab a horse and take off after Ned, who'd mounted up again and was galloping down the trail after the other Circle D riders, the back of his shirt still ablaze.

Longarm was about to take after them both when Dannenhower—coming alive suddenly—reached out, flung both arms around Longarm's legs, and with startling tenacity grappled him to the ground. The two men fought bitterly, each one seeking to throttle the other. As he tried to pull away, Longarm felt Dannenhower slip his .44 from its holster. He grabbed Dannenhower's wrist and tried to wrest the gun from his grasp. It detonated, the flash from the muzzle searing Longarm's cheek. Pulling away from the maddened cattleman, Longarm palmed his derringer and fired twice, point-blank, into the man's gut. Gasping, Dannenhower dropped Longarm's .44 and collapsed forward onto the ground.

Longarm picked up the gun and ran for his horse.

He came upon Ned, the man Johnny Danfield had taken after, ten minutes later. He was hanging from a cotton-wood limb. His Levi's were still smoking and a flap of roasted flesh had peeled off his right cheek. As Longarm rode closer, he heard a sound behind him. Turning in his saddle, he saw Johnny Danfield, astride a horse, close behind him, his rifle cocked and ready.

"Why'd you hang this man, Johnny?"

"I heard Frank Dannenhower call him Ned. His full name was Ned Swinnerton. He was on my list. Before I hung him, he admitted he was in the posse that killed my father."

"There was another one up here with him, I think. Pete something or other."

"That would be Pete Quirk. Where is he now, lawman?"

"He's dead. He was with Dannenhower and Ned Swinnerton when I shot him."

"*You* shot him? How come, lawman?"

"It's a long story."

Johnny Danfield glanced back. Smoke from the blazing kerosene was still pumping skyward, its black plumes visible above the trees. "What about Dannenhower?"

"Unless he can find a cattle spread in hell, he's finished with burning out ranches."

"Guess that's it, then."

"You going to hang me too, Johnny?"

"Nope."

"Why not?"

"You ain't on the list."

"There's two more you haven't caught up with yet."

"I know."

"You going after them?"

"I don't think so."

"Why not?"

"The doc took out one of the bullets you planted in me, lawman. The one in my chest, he couldn't find. I thought I was going to be all right. But that trouble this morning with Gulch and the kid told me different. I'm already coughing up parts of my lung, and I can feel the bullet moving in for the kill. I'm a dead man."

"I wish I could say I was sorry."

"That don't matter none. Right now, all I want is for you to leave me be. My grandma said it would be sweet for me to hunt down and hang them bastards who hung my pa. But it ain't been sweet, not at all."

"I met your grandma, Johnny, when I got that list."

"You mean she gave it to you?"

"No. She came on me after I found it in your desk."

Johnny shook his head in wonderment. "You're lucky she didn't kill you."

"She tried. But her heart gave out."

"Then she's dead."

Longarm nodded.

"It's over then. And I'm not sorry."

"I wish I could believe you mean that, Johnny."

"I do. Jesus Christ, man, I do."

Something in the man's voice convinced Longarm that Danfield was telling the truth. His macabre mission was over, even if it were not fully completed. His grandmother, watching from somewhere in hell, might be stomping in fury at his decision; but if the Devil was by her side, he'd be whispering in her ear to simmer down, that she had every reason to be proud of her terrible handiwork.

"All right, Johnny," Longarm said. "So long."

"Good-bye, lawman."

Johnny Danfield began to cough. It was a ragged, painful cough, and Longarm lifted his horse to a lope in order to escape it. He had not ridden far when he glanced back and saw that Johnny Danfield had joined Ned Swinnerton on the same cottonwood limb.

Longarm reached over for the bottle of Maryland rye and poured himself and Billy Vail another drink. They were standing at the bar in the Windsor Hotel. Longarm had been there some time, waiting for Billy Vail to show up. Now that he had, Longarm had a full confession to make—and a very serious request to put to his chief.

". . . so the thing is, Billy," Longarm finished,

"when I threw down on Frank Dannenhower and before that, when I shot Pete Quirk, I was taking the law into my own hands. And besides that, I made no effort to take Johnny Danfield in."

"No question about it," Vail drawled. "You done a real terrible thing. I'm real surprised at you, Custis." He belched.

"So maybe I ought to hang up the badge."

"Do what?"

"Put away the badge and try something else. There's a horse ranch up in Wyoming. I figure I might like to work it. That's real pretty country up there, Billy."

"Horse ranch my ass. If I'm any judge of your enthusiasms, Custis, there's a woman you met up there. She's what you're thinking of, not a corral full of horseflesh."

"Yeah," Longarm agreed. "And wait'll you see her."

"You invitin' me up, are you?"

"If you'll come."

"Longarm, will you please pour me another drink and shut up about raising horses? I promise you, your next assignment is going to be as far away from Wyoming Territory as I can make it."

"But I told you what I did, Chief."

"Sure, you told me. But let me ask you, did you stop this Johnny Danfield?"

Longarm filled Vail's shot glass. "I guess you could say I did."

"And did you save two of the men remaining on Danfield's list?"

"Yes."

"And you say you took out two of the bastards who shot down this doctor you deputized?"

"Yes, I did."

"Then I say you did good." Vail drained his glass of rye.

"You think so, Chief?"

"You want me to put it in writing? Now shut up and pass the bottle."

Longarm felt a hand on his shoulder, a warm, gentle hand. He turned. Betsy was standing behind him in a yellow gown cut so low he knew that as soon as she inhaled, she'd lose it, an event he was immediately looking forward to.

"Betsy? What the hell are you doing in Denver?"

"Do you know how much horse shit you have to shovel on a horse ranch? Do you know how *heavy* a shovelful of it is?"

He laughed. "I can imagine."

"No, you can't. I sold out to my barkeep and got me a lovely two-story home here in Denver. And I've just hired six of the loveliest girls."

"This calls for a celebration."

"Better than that. It calls for a visit."

Longarm introduced Betsy to Vail. She smiled warmly and shook his hand. Billy smiled back.

"When you do visit my new place," Betsy told

Longarm, "bring your friend here. I can see he appreciates a good thing when he sees it."

Vail chuckled and finished his drink. "I guess maybe you two'd be wanting to find a quiet booth and talk."

"No need for you to run off, Billy," Longarm said.

"Looks like I don't have no choice." Vail winked at Longarm. "There's a blizzard of paper on my desk come all the way from Washington. I might as well go up and clear it off. Thanks for the booze, Longarm—and hang on to that badge."

"I'll do that, Billy."

"Now," said Betsy, leading Longarm over to a booth, "I want to hear all about it—how you and the doc tracked down Johnny Danfield."

"Let me finish my drink first," he told her, sliding in beside her. "Then I'll get us a room upstairs. I'll tell you the whole story then. Afterwards, I mean. And thank you. Thank you very much."

She leaned closer and rested her hand on his thigh. "Aren't you thanking me a bit too soon?"

"Not at all. What I'm thanking you for is reminding me how much horse shit you have to shovel on a horse ranch."

She laughed and snuggled closer.

Watch for

LONGARM IN THE CLEARWATERS

one hundred thirty-first novel in the bold
LONGARM series from Jove

coming in November!

LONGARM

Explore the exciting Old West with
one of the men who made it wild!
